b l u e

## Build My Gallows High

GEOFFREY HOMES was the pen-name of writer Daniel Mainwaring. He was born in 1902 in California of an English father. After school at Fresno State College, he had a variety of jobs (clerk, fruit-picker, detective, salesman, teacher, journalist) before moving to Hollywood as a sound engineer and, later, PR for Warner Brothers studios and other majors.

His first novel, *One Against the Earth* (1933), was published under his own name, but his first venture into crime writing was with *The Doctor Died at Dusk*, under the Homes pseudonym (1936). This was the first of five novels featuring Robin Bishop, an investigative newspaperman. The last Bishop novel, *Then There Were Three* (1938), also featured his new character, the unconventional private detective Humphrey Campbell, who was then to enjoy four more novels on his own, together with his fat, lazy and corrupt partner Oscar Morgan.

But his most famous novel remains *Build My Gallows High* (1946) filmed by Jacques Tourneur as *Out of the Past* (1947) with Robert Mitchum, Kirk Douglas and Jane Greer, and again in 1984 by Taylor Hackford as *Against All Odds* with Jeff Bridges, James Woods and Rachel Ward.

This was also his last novel, as he became a sought-after Hollywood screenwriter. His film career was a prestigious one, including work with directors such as Joseph Losey, Anthony Mann, Jacques Tourneur, Don Siegel and many others. Films written by him include *The Lawless*, *Invasion of the Body Snatchers*, *Babyface Nelson*, *The Tall Target*, *Southwest Passage*, *East of Kilimanjaro*, *The Woman That Wouldn't Die* and 33 other movies.

Daniel Mainwaring died in 1978.

His other crime novels are *The Man who Murdered Himself*, *The Man Who Didn't Exist*, *The Man Who Murdered Goliath*, *No Hands on the Clock*, *Finders Keepers*, *Forty Whacks*, *The Street of the Crying Woman*, *The Hill of the Terrified Monk* and *Six Silver Handles*.

*Series Editor: Maxim Jakubowski*

# blue murder

Gil Brewer
*13 French Street & The Red Scarf*

David Goodis
*The Burglar*

Davis Grubb
*The Night of the Hunter*

Geoffrey Homes
*Build My Gallows High*

William P. McGivern
*The Big Heat*

Joel Townsley Rogers
*The Red Right Hand*

Newton Thornburg
*Cutter and Bone*

Charles Williams
*The Diamond Bikini*

Cornell Woolrich
*Rear Window & Other Stories*

*blue murder*

# BUILD MY GALLOWS HIGH

### Geoffrey Homes

# SIMON & SCHUSTER

**LONDON • SYDNEY • NEW YORK • TOKYO • TORONTO**

First published in 1946
First published as a Blue Murder paperback by
Simon & Schuster Limited 1988

© William Morrow and Company Inc. 1946

**Simon & Schuster Limited**
**West Garden Place, Kendal Street,**
**London W2 2AQ**

Simon & Schuster Australia Pty Limited
Sydney

---

British Library Cataloguing in Publication Data

---

Homes, Geoffrey, *1902–1978*
    Build my gallows high.
    Rn: Daniel Mainwaring    I. Title
813'.52 [F]

---

ISBN 0–671–65282–6

---

Phototypeset in Ehrhardt by Input Typesetting Ltd, London
Printed and bound in Great Britain by
Richard Clay Ltd, Bungay, Suffolk

# CHAPTER ONE

RED BAILEY didn't see her coming. He was squatting on the sand putting a McGinty and a black Gnat on his leader and the chatter of the creek covered the sound of her progress across the broad meadow. Now and then he looked up from the piece of wet gut to stare at the wall of mountains to the west. Patches of snow still scarred the smooth red shoulders and back toward Tioga Pass a fistful of clouds hung low. A light wind pushed through the willows along the creek and in a far pasture a calf was bawling. The shadow of a circling buzzard slid across the grass.

'Red,' the girl called. 'How do you get across this ditch?'

Red swung around, grinning. 'You wade.'

A ten-foot stretch of water lay between them. She hesitated momentarily, then shrugged and moved toward him through the knee-deep pool.

'A gentleman,' the girl said, when she reached the stretch of clean gray sand. 'That's what you are.' She was a slim girl in red shorts and a white silk shirt. She had a steel rod and a can of worms in her left hand.

'They biting?' She dropped down beside him. There she looked very small.

Red shook his head, flipped the leader in the shallow water. 'Too high.'

'Bait my hook.' She put the can in his lap.

'Bait it yourself.'

'I don't like it when they wiggle.' She wrinkled her small

1

nose at him. There was a net of freckles on the tip of it. 'When you going to marry me?'

'I'm not.' He spoke lightly, still smiling.

'Why?'

'Unworthy,' Red said.

'I don't think so.'

'You don't know,' Red said. He ran the line through the eyelets of her pole, took a leader from his fly hook and tied it on the line.

'Bailey the mysterious.' She watched his nimble fingers slide a fat worm on the hook. Her glance moved up and searched his strong, almost ugly face.

'There you are.' Red gave her the rod. She put it on the sand but made no move to rise. Back of them the sun slid close to the ridge and the shadows grew long on the meadow. Suddenly she said sharply, 'I don't care what you've done, or what you are.'

He stared back at her and his eyes were full of darkness. 'Ann,' he said softly.

'Oh, Red.' She moved closer to him and put her hands on his big shoulders.

'It wouldn't work, Ann.'

Her lips stopped the words. She clung to him awkwardly. The wind tore a leaf from a willow and dropped it at their feet. The shadow of the mountains crawled nearer, darkening the water as it swirled by, tugging at the reeds.

'It would,' Ann said. 'It would, Red.'

'No.' The word was unsure.

'You love me. You said so.'

'That has nothing to do with it.'

'What has, then?'

'I told you.'

'Told me?' she scoffed. 'What? Go on. In the first place, I'm too young. Twenty is too young.'

'Much too young.'

'And you're too old.'

'Much too old. And too beat up around the edges.'

'With a past,' Ann said. 'A black past. And maybe a wife somewhere.'

'No wife. But a past.'

'Your name isn't Red Bailey?'

'No.'

'You were a detective and you did something.'

'Right.'

'But you won't say what.'

'No.'

'So you went to Korea and became a hero.'

'Not exactly,' Red said.

'You fought.'

'And bled.'

'For a principle.'

'Of necessity.'

'You believed.'

'Eventually. I get no credit for that. I'm not altogether stupid.'

'Then you came to Bridgeport and opened a gas station.'

He pulled a pack of cigarettes from a jacket pocket, lit one for her, one for himself.

'I came along –' Ann went on, blowing smoke at him. 'I came along to confuse you.'

Red lay back. A weary bit of moon was almost lost in the waste of pale sky. Her small hand touched his cheek. He caught it and kissed the palm, thinking, *sometimes I'm not confused. Sometimes when it's like this I know it would work.*

He turned his head a little and then he could see the mountains he loved – not red any more because the sun was gone. Up there were pine-fringed lakes and brawling streams and deep drifts of snow.

She stretched out close to him, pillowing her head on his arm. 'I could go away. Do you want me to go away?'

'No,' Red said softly.

'Nothing matters but us, does it?'

'No.'

'And it will work out, won't it?'

3

'Yes.' At that moment, he was sure of it. The past was dead. Ten years dead, and buried deep.

But two hours later, when Ann Miller stopped her father's Packard at the curb in front of Bailey's One Stop Service Station on the outskirts of town, Red Bailey wasn't so sure. A battered Dodge parked alongside the station. Sitting under the wheel was the little Greek, Joe Stefanos.

The little Greek wore a white linen suit and a Panama hat of incongruous size. He slid out of the car and stood there, smoking a cigarette in a long ivory holder, watching Red come across the gravel.

'Good evening,' Stefanos said.

'Hello.' Red went past him into the station where the Kid was repairing a tire.

The Kid wiped his dirty hands on a piece of waste, jerked his thumb toward the Dodge. He had the wizened, starved face of a jockey and a peculiar, crooked scar crossed his narrow forehead. Red didn't know how old he was. The Kid had dropped off a Reno-bound truck a couple of years before and had stuck around ever since. He was deaf and dumb.

'I'll take over,' Red said, facing the Kid and forming the words to make it easier for him to understand. 'You run along.'

The Kid's nimble fingers asked a question. 'Any fish?'

'Water's too high yet. Beat it. This guy wants to talk to me.'

The Kid went across the yard giving the Greek the eye. As he went past, Stefanos flipped his cigarette away and spat after him.

'Come on in,' Red called. Bending, he opened the register and slid a revolver in the hip pocket of his jeans.

'Nice little place.' Stefanos had a smooth, high voice that seldom varied its pitch. His lips smiled. His heavy-lidded, protuberant eyes didn't. He looked over one shoulder at the sign swinging in the wind, and added, Mr. Bailey.'

'I like it.'

'Don't that dummy make you nervous?'

4

'Silence has its points,' Red said. 'What do you want?' He leaned against the wall, looking down at the other man.

'Me? Nothing.'

'Just a social call?'

'Sort of.'

Red waited, his big knobby face set, his eyes dark and brooding.

'Guy,' said the little Greek, 'he wants to see you.'

'He still alive?'

Stefanos nodded.

'Why?' Red asked.

The little Greek grinned. 'You can ask him.' He nodded toward the sign. 'Why the name change?'

Red shrugged. 'Tired of the old one.'

'Strange racket to find you in, Mr. Bailey.'

'Nice and quiet,' Red said. 'And the fishing's good. What does Guy want?'

'He's got a job for you.'

'I've one here.'

'This is a good one.'

'No, thanks.'

'I think you should talk to him.'

Red shook his head. 'Not interested.'

'He said you were to come back with me.' The little Greek took his right hand out of his jacket pocket. There was a gun in it. It was a thirty-eight with a stubby barrel.

'So that's how it is!' Red said mildly. 'All right. Put it away.'

'You'll come?'

'Where is he?'

'Reno. The El Arbol.'

'I'll be up in a couple of days.'

'He wants you right away.'

'Tomorrow then. I'll drive up in the morning.'

'I said right away.'

Red opened the cash register, took out some bills and

shoved them in a pocket. He scribbled a note to the Kid and put it in the drawer. 'How do I get back?'

The little Greek smiled. 'That will be taken care of.'

Red cocked his head. 'Or do I come back?'

'Of course,' the little Greek said.


Ann Miller lived in a big, white farmhouse two miles east of the town, where the highway to Reno swung sharply north. Behind it the meadow land was threaded with small streams that were angry now the snow was melting. Old man Miller's herd of Hereford bulls grazed in the east pasture and made trespassing inadvisable. A stretch of lawn lay in front of the house and a row of populars stood on the windward side.

'That's it,' Red said. The little Greek swung the car off the highway and slammed on the brakes. The car slid to a stop.

'Step on it,' Stefanos said.

Red got out of the car and moved unhurriedly through the gate and up the path. Ann's mother opened the door for him. She was lean, angular and unhappy. Red's presence on the porch didn't cheer her up. She stood aside without speaking. Red went in.

Ann's father was stretched out in a leather chair with his shoes off, reading the paper. He looked up and nodded sourly.

'Evening.'

'Hello, Mr. Miller.' Red wondered if Ann would be like her father and mother in a few years. That, he decided, would be too bad. At the foot of the hall stairway Mrs. Miller paused and called whiningly: 'Ann. It's Mr. Bailey.'

He heard the rush of her feet on the landing. She came running down, her face shining and happy. As she caught her father's glance, she moved less precipitously. It was evident the Millers did not approve of their daughter's choice. A girl as well educated and mannered, as shapely as Ann, could certainly do much better than tag around with a

6

tough, red-haired giant of forty-two, with a crooked nose and one shoulder higher than the other.

'All pressed up,' Ann said. Her glance sobered.

Red nodded toward the porch.

'You going out?' Mrs. Miller asked.

'No,' Red said and led the way outside. The girl pulled the door to behind her.

It was growing dark outside. A whole field of stars had suddenly ripened and through it swung the thin sickle of the moon. In the fields the frogs were singing. Red moved to the end of the porch, staring across the darkening meadow. Back of the barn a nighthawk cried out. Ann came close to him and her fingers dug into his arm.

She pressed against him and he could feel a firm breast against his arm.

'You'll come back?'

'Sure,' Red said.

'Trouble?'

'Business.'

'You scared hell out of me for a minute.'

'Your father will hear you.'

'Let him.'

'He doesn't like me. He thinks I'm a bad influence.'

'Aren't you?'

'I'm better for you than the game warden,' Red said. 'But they like him. Stay away from him while I'm gone.'

'Red.' Her voice was very low.

'Yes?'

'You've made up your mind?'

'Yes.'

'Oh, Red.'

The blast of a horn silenced the frog song, went echoing across the fields.

He kissed her. 'I'll be back. Maybe tomorrow night. I've decided – to hell with the past. To hell with everything but us.' He held her face in his hands. It seemed to him her eyes found a whole handful of stars and held them.

7

'I love you, Ann.' With that he was gone.

She moved to the edge of the porch and watched him hurry down the path and through the gate, saw him round the dark bulk of the waiting car, heard the door slam. The motor roared, the lights went on and the car shot out into the highway. She waited until its red light disappeared around the bend and then she turned. Suddenly all the laughter left her and the night seemed very cold. He was gone and she was sure she would never see him again.

# CHAPTER TWO

A COUPLE of miles beyond Virginia City the little Greek swung the car from the state highway into a graveled side road and headed east. The night was going, the wisp of moon long since down and the stars fading. The ribbon of dawn stretched taut across the eastern sky. Stefanos yawned, ran his tongue over his teeth. 'Awake?' he asked.

'Sure,' Red said.

'Here we are.'

'Not bad.' Red stretched. Ahead was a cotton-wood-bordered lane leading up a little hill. On the hill sat El Arbol Rancho, two-storied, gleaming white, with a pillared porch and great chimneys. Limousines stood bumper to bumper along the circular driveway, their drivers dozing at the wheels. Lights blazed inside.

'And all on the up and up,' the little Greek said.

'Not that,' Red said.

'This is Nevada.' The Dodge rocketed up the hill and around the drive. Stefanos jammed on the brakes, got out. Red followed, stood on the broad steps, stretching. A big Negro in a purple uniform came toward them.

'Put it away,' the little Greek ordered. The Negro gave him a dirty look. They crossed the porch and the door swung open. A man with a paunch took Red apart with his eyes. Red needed a couple of minutes to place him. That was because he was wearing a dinner coat instead of the ratty blue serge most plain clothesmen wore. He gave Red a bleak smile and said, 'Hello, you big bastard.'

'Did he bring the whole force with him?' Red asked, taking Mac's proffered flabby hand.

Mac whinnied. 'Just the honest ones.'

'You short-handed?'

Mac whinnied again. 'Same old Red. What's cooking?'

'Me,' Red said, and followed Stefanos across the circular hallway and up a broad flight of stairs. The carpet was deep red. Shrill laughter and a hum of voices welled up after him. The little Greek led him down a long hall and through a heavy door.

Guy Parker sat behind a desk big enough to sleep two. He was playing solitaire and he was thinner than Red remembered – a slab of a man with gray hair and a razor face. On the paneled wall behind him stood a framed photograph. Guy was the central figure in the picture. He wore the uniform of a police chief and he was shaking hands with Herbert Hoover. Hoover had his other hand in his pants pocket as though he was keeping track of his watch.

'Well, well, well!' Guy exclaimed, getting up and making the portage around the desk. 'Old Red himself. How they treating you, boy?'

'Fair enough.' They shook hands. Guy's fist was a piece of cold iron.

'Long time, Red.'

'Ten, eleven years.'

'You've been around some.'

'Some.'

'How come you folded your office?'

'Did you get me up here to ask that?'

Guy chuckled. 'Same old Red.'

'Or haven't you got enough detective talent around the joint?' Red wasn't smiling.

'Small caliber,' Guy said. 'Very small.'

The little Greek cut in. 'I'm going to bed.'

Guy ignored him and the little Greek went out.

10

'Sweet character,' Red said. 'I always expected him to die young.' Without being asked, he sat down. Guy went back to his deck of cards. He shuffled clumsily.

'So you're selling gas.'

'When did you find that out?'

'A while back.'

'How?'

'We use that road a lot.'

'All right,' Red said. 'Spill it. What do you want?'

'I've got a job for you.'

Red shook his head.

'Hear me out,' Guy started dealing. He dealt two hands of ten cards each, put the rest of the deck on the desk, upturned the top card, indicated the other hand. Red pulled his chair up, picked up the cards and arranged them. He had four kings, three treys, a pair of eights and a jack. The card on the desk was an eight. Red exchanged it for the jack, put his hand down. 'Gin.'

'How do you like that!' Guy said. He collected the cards, re-shuffled them. 'You were a good one – you know that, Red.'

'Sure.'

'No better.'

'Deal from the top.' Red said. 'This isn't for dough. Anyway, it's my deal.' Guy gave him the deck.

'Still good?'

'I wouldn't know.'

'A man doesn't forget his trade.'

'Maybe not.'

'This is a sweet job.' Guy kept his eyes on Red's long, supple fingers as they flipped the cards out. 'You go to New York, you get a line on a boy and there you are.'

'Where?' Red lit a cigarette, stared through the smoke at the card faces.

'With five grand.'

'I'd rather pump gas.'

'What's got into you? There was a time –' Guy let the sentences trail off into nothingness.

'Yes,' Red said. 'There was.'

'A pushover.' Guy took a card, discarded a queen. 'For you, that is. Take maybe two weeks.'

Red picked up the queen, discarded a ten.

'One,' Red said and put down his hand.

'Got me for twenty-five.'

'I was dealing.'

'A pushover,' Guy repeated. 'Trip to New York. All expenses and five grand. You can't kiss that off.'

'Can't I?' Red fiddled with the cards, waiting. He didn't like the setup, didn't like it at all. Guy Parker didn't play unless the deck was stacked. But he couldn't know. He would have moved in a long time ago.

'Two weeks – maybe three,' Guy said.

'Maybe I'm out of practice.'

'I'll take that chance.'

'There are good boys in the East, Guy.'

'Not good enough. Anyway, I can't trust someone I don't know.'

'I don't get it,' Red said in a flat voice. 'Why come to me? I've been out of business ten years. Sure, I was good once. But I'm out of touch with things. In that racket, you need contacts.'

Guy pursed his thin lips. 'It's this way, Red. You've been out of the picture a long time. That's good. I want someone nobody knows.' He nodded thoughtfully. 'Someone with a clean slate.'

'There are plenty of honest agencies.'

'Don't give me that,' Guy said.

'Who's the boy you want a line on?'

'His name won't mean anything to you.'

'Try me.'

'Lloyd Eels,' Guy said.

Red shook his head.

'He's an attorney,' Guy went on. 'He's been sniping at a friend of mine. I want to stop him.'

'And your friend?'

'Never mind him.'

'I don't go into things blind.'

'What do you care?'

'I'm living the kind of life I like. I'm too old to want excitement any more.'

Red stood up. 'Got someone to take me home?'

'Sure. If you want to go.'

'I want to.'

'Stick around,' Guy said. 'Get some sleep and think it over.'

'No, thanks.'

'All right then.' Guy sighed and put his finger on a button. A voice came out of the little speaker on his desk. 'Yes, boss?' the voice inquired.

'Send the dame on in,' Guy spoke into the instrument. 'I want her to meet a friend of mine before he leaves.' He gave Red a thin smile.

Red stood there looking at him, his face expressionless. Faintly the sound of motors starting came to them. The customers had had enough and were going home. The door behind him opened. Red turned. Mumsie McGonigle came through the door.

Mumsie McGonigle and Red Bailey stood looking at each other, not smiling, not saying anything. The same serene wisp of a woman.

'I needn't introduce you,' Guy said.

'Not us,' Red said.

'Mumsie's working for me now.' Guy was standing at his desk, leaning on his knuckles. Red wondered where he bought his suits. The gray flannel he wore looked very British.

'That's fine,' Red said.

'You're working for me too.' Guy sounded like a cop for

the first time. Sure of himself. Very sure of himself. 'I'm being fair about it. Not asking for a cut. Not asking for anything but a little of your time, Red.'

Mumsie spoke. She had a low, sweet voice. 'I didn't sell you out, Red.'

'No?'

'No. Damned if I know how he got onto it.'

'Christ,' Guy said. 'I was chief of police, wasn't I?'

Mumsie's lying, Red thought. No other answer. He knew and she knew and that was all. Nobody else mixed up in it. No loose ends. He wasn't angry. He wasn't surprised. He asked: 'What did he get on you to make you talk, Mumsie?'

Guy answered for her. 'This and that.'

'I didn't –' Mumsie started to say. Red's eyes stopped her. She shrugged, moved to the leather couch against the wall and sat down. Her legs were still good.

'I'm not sore. Just curious.'

'He knows the works.' Mumsie lit a cigarette.

Guy nodded, moved to a cabinet in the corner and got a bottle of Scotch and some glasses. 'Want me to put a tombstone on his grave for you?' he asked.

'Mumsie should do that,' Red said.

Her voice found anger. 'I didn't kill him.'

Guy brought the bottle and glasses back to the desk. He poured three slugs and held one out to Red. Red crossed and took the glass. Guy went over to Mumsie and gave her one.

Red downed the drink. 'When do you want me to leave?'

'There's a train at four.' Guy sat down beside Mumsie.

'I'll catch some sleep then.'

'Six is vacant. Upstairs to the right. How about breakfast?'

'That can wait.'

'Sleep well, Mr. Markham,' Guy said.

'I like Bailey better,' Red said. He smiled at Mumsie and went out.

14

# CHAPTER THREE

*He lay there watching the sun come up, not able to sleep because there was too much to think about. There was Ann and there was Guy Parker, who had him where the hair was short. He tried to keep his mind on Ann. But she became misty, unreal. Out of his life now. Out of it for good. When Guy got his hooks into you, that was that. He thought about Mumsie and wondered if she had changed much inside. A strange dame Mumsie. His mind went back ten years:*

IT STARTED to snow when Red came up out of the subway. He turned the collar of his camel's-hair coat up around his ears, shoved his hands deep in the pockets and headed for his office, wondering why in hell he bothered coming to work, why he didn't turn the joint over to his partner and hop a train west or south – it didn't matter where. Just so there was sun. Passing a line of shivering, shabby men in front of a soup kitchen, he stopped pitying himself. He hurried past, felt their dull glances following him and even when he pushed through the doors into the warm shelter of the dingy office building he felt the hopeless envy of those rheumy eyes.

The blonde at the cigar counter tried with a smile to brighten his day.

'Morning, Mr. Markham,' the blonde said.

He returned the smile, stopped long enough to buy a pack of Virginia Rounds and make a few unenthusiastic verbal passes. Then he stepped into the waiting elevator and let it carry him slowly and painfully up six floors.

The elevator smelled of moth crystals. So did everything else in the place. When the windows of the building were open, the sharp scent of the crystals was almost overpowering. Even when the windows were closed, you could still taste the stuff. There was no escaping it short of moving out of the wholesale fur district. You talked about moving. You considered taking a suite in some modern office building farther uptown. But you kept putting it off, for some reason or another. Anyway, most of your clients were such crumbs that you rather welcomed the smell drifting up from the narrow street.

'Cold out – ain't it, Mr. Markham?' the elevator operator said.

Red admitted it was. He dusted powdery snow off his shoulders.

'Kids like it,' the elevator operator said. 'Kids can slide. Me, I ain't got a sled.'

'I'll lend you mine,' Red said. The doors opened. He stepped across the hall, fumbling for his keys. The gesture was unnecessary. The door, whose frosted glass informed the world that Peter Markham and Jack Fisher, Private Investigators, held forth inside was unlocked.

The small reception room was empty. From beyond the door leading into the office he shared with Fisher came a girl's silly giggle. Mr. Fisher was in, apparently. And Mr. Fisher was starting early. Red coughed as he crossed to the door then pushed it open.

Fisher and the redhead grinned at him embarrassedly, moved a few inches farther apart.

'Good way as any to keep warm,' Red said. 'Both of you fix your lipstick. It's on crooked.' He left the door open and went over to his desk.

'You might at least say good morning,' the redhead pouted. A green sweater was stretched tight across her big, high-

16

pointed breasts. Red wondered if it was the chest that inspired his partner's yen for the girl.

'Good morning, my pet,' Red said. 'Good morning, Jackson.'

'We have a client.' Fisher scrubbed his lips with a crumpled handkerchief.

'Your wife?' Red dropped into his worn leather chair and propped his feet on the desk.

Fisher scowled at him. 'Little early to be so full of quips.'

Red waved at the door. 'Back to the treadmill, Gertrude.' She smoothed her skirt over her hips, batted her eyelashes at him and slithered out.

'I'd be happier if she could spell,' Red said. 'But anything to keep you content, Jackson.'

'Stop riding me – I get enough of that at home. I said we had a client.'

'What do you want me to do – cheer?'

'You might show some interest in the business.'

'It has ceased to fascinate me,' said Red. 'And I have no yen for Gertrude to brighten my day.'

Fisher ignored the remark. He gave Red a name. 'Whit Sterling.'

'What about him?'

'He's the client.'

'Somebody welch on him?'

'Would he call us in for that?'

Red shook his head. 'Just let me keep guessing.'

'Go ahead,' said Fisher. 'I don't know what he wants us for. All I know is he called and said to come on over.'

'Probably lost one of his dogs.' Red didn't move.

'You gettin' choosy?' Fisher grumbled. 'Christ, let's see what he wants!'

'Leave us stick to good clean work like following husbands around,' said Red. 'Mr. Sterling plays too rough.'

'You ain't scared of him –' sneered Fisher, 'not Red Markham?'

'Scared to death,' said Red cheerfully.

17

'Me, I got responsibilities,' Fisher argued. 'Here's a chance to pick up some dough. A chance to keep on eating.'

Red leaned his chin on his fists and eyed his chubby, balding partner. 'You don't look hungry.'

'Give me time. The way things have been going it won't be long.'

'Tighten your belt,' said Red. 'Stay out of bars and give up Gertrude. Patronize the soup kitchens.'

The telephone snarled. Red picked up the receiver.

'Yes,' he admitted, 'this is Markham. All right. Put him on.'

Whit Sterling's thin voice said, 'Hello, you big red bastard. Get on over here.'

'Why?' asked Red.

'Because it's snowing.' The thin voice got even thinner. 'Because I think you need a vacation.'

'When did you start worrying about my health?' Red asked.

'A couple of days ago,' the voice replied. 'When a dame put a thirty-two slug in my tummy. Now be a good boy and come on over, because this is something I cannot discuss with the Johns. Not and keep their respect.'

Fisher had moved over and was standing above him.

'Christ, say yes!' Fisher urged. Red looked up at him, shrugged.

'All right,' Red said. 'We'll be over.'

'Thanks.' The voice died. Red put the receiver on the hook, lighted a cigarette, and stood up. 'But against my better judgment, Jackson. And only because I don't want Gertrude to suffer.'

'A card,' said Fisher as he put on his coat. 'That's what you are – a card.'

The angry wind threw snow against the windows of Whit Sterling's apartment on the seventeenth floor of a house on Fifty-Seventh Street. Out there in the mist was the East River and a tugboat complained mournfully as it headed north. Sterling lay under a tufted quilt and the pink silk made his cheeks pinker than ever. He had a fine head of black hair and a thin mustache. The mild young man who let Red and Fisher in went back to the chair beside the bed and sat down. He was holding a copy of *North of Boston* and his forefinger marked his place in the book of poems.

'Take your coats off and sit down,' Sterling said. 'Lou, break out the Scotch.'

'Too early,' said Red.

'Speak for yourself,' said Fisher. 'I could use a drink.'

Wearily the mild young man got up, put his book on the chair and went into the other room. Red indicated the book.

'Lou was reading to me,' Sterling said. 'How you been, Red?'

'Fair, Whit.'

'Business good?'

'Lousy. And yours?'

'Average.'

The man named Lou returned with Fisher's drink, gave it to him grudgingly and resumed his seat. 'Don't talk anymore,' he told Sterling.

Sterling's head relaxed on the pillow. There were lines of bitterness around his mouth and his eyes were clouded with pain.

'Somebody has to talk,' Red observed. 'This is no social call.' Fisher shot a pained looked at him.

'Mr. Sterling wants you to find a young woman for him,' Lou explained.

'I thought he might,' said Red. 'Mr. Sterling is not the forgiving type. Why did she shoot him?'

'That's unimportant,' Lou brushed the question aside.

'Except to Whitney,' grinned Red. 'Eh, Whit?'

Sterling's expression hardened. He wet his lips and his lids lowered over his eyes.

'Her name is Mumsie McGonigle,' Lou went on in his cool, precise voice. 'After the shooting she disappeared. So did fifty-six thousand dollars.'

19

Fisher looked up from his drink, whistled softly. Lou gave him a disapproving glance.

'A police case,' Red observed.

Sterling spoke without opening his eyes. 'No. Yours.'

'So that's how it was,' said Red.

'We're not asking you to think.' Lou took a wallet from his pocket, extracted five one-thousand-dollar bills and held them out to Red. 'Find her. Bring her back here and forget it.'

'You want her, or the dough?' Red asked, ignoring the proffered bills.

'Both.'

'And what happens to her?'

'Nothing.'

Red's look had disbelief in it. Lou smiled. 'She left under the impression she had killed Mr. Sterling,' said Lou. 'Naturally she was frightened.'

'And her conscience hurt her,' Red said.

Sterling opened his eyes. They were as warm as a cat's. 'My gut keeps me from laughing. Will you get busy?'

Through the smoke of his cigarette, Red grinned at the man under the pink quilt. 'Tell me more about Mumsie, Whitney.'

'He shouldn't be talking,' Lou protested.

Sterling ignored the protest, adjusted his pillow so that he could look across at Red, gingerly touched his stomach. 'I had it coming. She found me with another dame. I want her back.' He motioned to Lou. 'Show him her picture. Then maybe the bastard will believe me.'

Languidly Lou crossed to the dresser, opened the top drawer, took out a photograph and, returning, handed it to Red. He stood over the detective, holding the wad of money in his right hand.

Red stared at the lovely oval face. After a moment he turned his attention back to Sterling. 'I'd want her back too,' he admitted. 'But then, I'm a sentimentalist. I never suspected you of tender moments, Whit.'

20

Fisher spoke for the first time. 'For Christ's sake,' he said, 'don't you ever run down?'

'He's having fun.' Sterling offered Red a thin smile. 'Five thousand now and another five when you bring her back. Plus expenses.'

'And God help Mumsie.' Red flicked the picture with his forefinger.

Whit shook his head. 'I won't touch her.'

'Any idea where she went?'

'Mexico, probably. I took her there last year and she loved it. Anyway, that's where I'd suggest looking.'

Across the bed Red could see the windows. He could see the snow flaking down and could hear the wind petulantly rattling the glass. There would be sun in Mexico – sun and a warm wind, orchids in the jungle and a sky washed clean of clouds.

Reaching out, he took the money from Lou's hand and thrust it carelessly in a pocket. He stood above the bed, dribbling smoke from his thin nostrils.

'A deal, Whit. On one condition. You don't lay a hand on her and none of your boys lays a hand on her.'

'I said that already.'

'I'll see you after a while.' Red headed for the door, opened it, threw a bleak smile back at Sterling and went out. Fisher hurried after him.

At the elevator Fisher held out one hand. 'Come on – give!'

Red gave him two one-thousand-dollar bills. 'Wrap Gertude in mink,' he suggested. 'And start checking railroad stations.'

'What are you going to do?'

'Pack,' Red said.

*The door creaked. He didn't look toward it, but he knew who was there. He knew Mumsie was looking at him. He kept his eyes on the window and pretended to be asleep. Beyond the barren, brown hills the Sierras were like ghosts of mountains.*

*There had been mountains in Mexico-great, towering cones of mountains. There had been plateaus patched crookedly with cane fields and there had been the lacy hem of the warm blue sea in Acapulco Bay. The lock clicked. Mumsie's soft footsteps went away. He closed his eyes, remembering:*

There was a little cafe named La Mar Azul, half a block from La Marina Hotel in Acapulco. It faced the plaza and on Saturday nights it was a fine place to sit and drink beer and listen to the band. Then it was very crowded. But on other nights it had plenty of room. Red used to drop in and sit there, watching the domino players, listening to the click of the ivory pieces and the soft voices, hearing the loud speaker on the theater around the corner. Late at night, when he lay in his hot room on the sixth floor of the hotel, the brassy music of the speaker was bad. But he didn't mind it in the cafe.

The cafe was open to the world. Kids kept threading their way between the tables, trying to sell lottery tickets and postcards, or offering to shine your shoes for ten centavos. They bothered Red a lot at first. After a while they took it for granted he was not a tourist. So they let him alone.

And after a while the little boys who wanted to show you the town for fity centavos gave him up as a bad job too. That first week, when he wandered through the hot little town, they were always at his heels, pleading, smiling, tugging at his coat. But presently he could walk unmolested. He used to move slowly through the dusk, past the open air markets where you could buy a pair of huaraches for a peso and a hat for ten centavos, where you could get a meal for a tostan from a woman squatting by her charcoal brazier.

It was very hot that time. In the afternoons Acapulco slept. On the long crescent of beach to the south the people drowsed under yellow and green umbrellas. A few brown kids paddled in the warm water. No one swam much. Red did.

He liked that water, so heavy with salt you could lie for

hours on top of it, clean and blue and warm. You could lie and watch the odd cloud patterns on the bleached sky.

He had been there three weeks when he saw Mumsie. He was in La Mar Azul and she came along the street and stood in front of the place, staring in as though searching for someone. She flicked Red with a glance. Her gaze moved to the empty table near him and she walked slowly to it and sat down. She put her hands on the table and looked at them.

Red wasn't the only one there who saw her. Every man in the place relaxed his attention from the game he was playing and watched her. There was a good reason. She was a slim, lovely little thing with eyes too big for her face and the serene look often seen on nuns. She wore a white linen dress and a hat of fine staw, as pale as her hair. The players gave her more warm looks from their dark eyes, shrugged and went back to their games. A lone woman, but an American. So that made it all right. Americans were odd. In Acapulco you saw so many of them you got used to their peculiarities.

Red didn't speak to her that night. He wanted to. He wanted to smile at her and move to the chair across the table so that he could see the color of her eyes. He thought they must be blue – pale blue like the sky over the bay.

But they weren't blue. Red found that out the next night. The loud speaker on the front of the theater was braying and across the plaza some guy was keeping his hands on the horn of an automobile. The horn played three notes. The domino players didn't mind. One of them was a policeman but he didn't do anything about the horn.

She came along the sidewalk and this time she didn't look at anyone. She merely went to the same table and sat down. He heard her low, sweet voice asking the waiter for a brandy and plain water. He caught her eyes and grinned. A ghost of a smile crossed her face. He asked: 'May I?' She dropped her glance.

The waiter brought her drink. Red beckoned to him, asked for another beer and when it came watched her over the top of the tall glass. The dress she were tonight was of some soft

23

green stuff, but her hat was the same and her shoes and her bag matched the hat. She took a black notebook from her bag and began writing in it with a tiny gold pencil. As she wrote she pulled her eyebrows together and pursed her full lips. Her lips were very red and made her skin seem paler than it really was.

A ragged boy crossed from the plaza and headed straight for her table. His soft voice begged for just one little centavo – *please senorita, just one*. She smiled at the flat, dirty brown face. Surely, the boy continued in Spanish, the senorita could spare one tiny centavo.

She looked at Red then. She spoke. 'What does he say?'

'He wants a cent,' Red said. Red waved him away – told him to run along before he cut his ears off. The boy laughed and took some lottery tickets from his pocket.

'The senorita will win a fortune perhaps,' the boy suggested.

Red got up, moved to her table, gave him a fifty-centavo piece and took one of the tickets.

'*Gracias, senor,*' the boy said.

'*Por nada.*'

'Which means?' she asked.

'For nothing,' Red said, as the boy went away. 'May I sit down?'

'Yes.'

'Thank you.'

'*Por nada.*' She smiled and a light seemed to go on in her eyes. They were light brown, flecked with bits of gold, and her long lashes made shadows on her fine pale skin.

'I wanted to speak to you last night,' Red said.

'I know.'

'You looked lonely.'

'I'm not. Was that why you wanted to speak to me?'

'No. I wanted to ask you to walk along the beach in the moonlight. I wanted to sit beside you on a hill.'

'You're the lonely one.' She smiled again. Red wanted her

24

to keep smiling – she was even lovelier then. 'I don't know your name.'

'Does that matter?' Red asked.

'Yes.'

'They call me Red.'

'How odd,' the girl laughed softly. 'Red what?'

'Markham. And yours?'

She shook her head. 'You wouldn't believe it. Why are you in Acapulco?'

'I like it.'

'Tourist?'

'Indolent,' Red said. 'This is a fine place to be indolent in.'

'Even if you're lonely?'

'I'm not lonely any more.' He reached across the table and covered her hand with his own. 'They have a fine bar at the El Mirador. Shall we walk up the hill and have a drink?'

'Not tonight.'

'Tomorrow then?'

'Tomorrow afternoon. Say four.'

'You won't run away?'

'No.'

'Thank you.'

'*Por nada.*' She said the words as though she liked the sound and her voice did things to Red's stomach.

El Mirador made Red think of Carmel – the hotel hanging on the edge of the cliff, the rocks and the sea and the sky. They sat at a table, high above the water. On the cliff below two boys chased an iguana. After a while they caught him and came clambering up the rocks, one of them holding the ugly thing by the tail. The girl shuddered. She asked, 'Why?'

'To eat,' Red said. He was glad when they were gone. Then there were only the cliffs and the sea gnawing at the rocks far down and two buzzards riding an air current low over the blue-green water. 'This isn't Mexico,' Red said.

'Oh yes.' She sipped her daiquiri, leaned on the porch

railing and nodded at the buzzards wheeling by. 'They're Mexico. I've seen them by the dozens roosting in the dead trees along the road. I've seen them everywhere. They're always with you, like –' She cut the sentence off and there was darkness in her eyes.

'Like what?'

'Death,' the girl said, staring across at him.

The shadows of the birds slid across the rocks. 'I know a place where there are only the cliffs and the sea,' Red said. 'White sand. White and clean. The rocks shut out everything but the sky and the sea. There's nothing to make you think of death.'

Mumsie rose. 'Show it to me,' she said softly.

Not far away the waves gnawed hungrily at the rocks. They lay in shadow on the warm sand and high above them hung one lost and lonely cloud. Mumsie sat up and watched the water running up the beach, stopping to push the smooth, white pebbles around a bit with cool white fingers, then drawing away. Presently she turned and stared down at Red. His head was pillowed in his hands.

'When do we go back, Red?' she asked suddenly.

Red's glance rested on her face. He took one of her hands. 'There's no hurry. He didn't die.'

'Oh.'

'He wants you back.'

'So you'll take me?'

'I've been thinking about things.'

With her free hand she made patterns in the sand. Red pulled himself up beside her, slid one arm around her shoulders.

'I could tell him you hopped a boat,' Red said. 'I could tell him you had lost yourself in Panama or Chile. Anywhere. That I'm not bloodhound enough to pick up your trail.'

'Would he believe you?'

'I'll chance it.'

'Then what?'

'You and I,' Red said softly.

'He'd find us. You don't know him like I do, Red.'

Red grinned. 'I don't want to. What about it?'

'I can't go back.'

'No. And maybe he doesn't want you back after all. Maybe he wants his fifty-six thousand bucks.'

She threw him a puzzled glance. 'Fifty-six thousand? Is that what he said?' Red nodded. 'So that's why you'll take a chance on me?'

'We'll give it back to him. I'll say I found you and talked you out of the dough but couldn't persuade you to come back.'

'I didn't take that much money,' Mumsie said. 'Not anywhere near that much. He lied to you. I took enough to get me here. There's very little left.'

'All the better, then.' His arm tightened about her. 'You can't accuse me of being greedy.'

'No. Only of being foolish.' She shrugged his arm away, stood up and moved down the sand. The waves swept up the beach and drove her back. Without turning she spoke. 'All you know about me is I lived with a gambler and when he got tired of me I shot him and ran away.'

Red rose to stand beside her. 'That's not all.'

'What else?'

'A moment.'

'Is that enough?'

'Yes.' He pulled her closer, tilted her face with one forefinger and kissed her. The waves reached out for them, drew back, reached out again. Far above, the tidy wind swept the lonely cloud away behind the hills.

*You got over things like love and death. The thought was somehow frightening when you knew that one of these days Ann might get over you. But you couldn't deny it, couldn't say, 'Hell, it won't happen to us.'*

*Mumsie had come along the hall and had opened the door a while ago. There was a time when he would have been almost*

27

*breathless waiting for her to come to him, waiting for her lips, her breasts and her body.*

*Yes, he had rid himself of desire but he had taken a beating doing it. Love for her was long since dead or, rather, love for the woman he had imagined was dead.*

*At first he hadn't loved her. Those weeks in Acapulco — the nights hot and still until a morning wind came along, the days bright with Mexican voices that were like cricket songs — he had wanted her as he had wanted no other woman in his life. But he saw the imperfections — a smallness, a stinginess, a tendency to give grudgingly or not at all of everything but her body.*

*It was on the boat wallowing amiably north that he had stopped seeing clearly. Mumsie became something he made up — not a beautiful woman who had put a lead slug in Whit Sterling's belly. It had taken a good kick in the teeth to bring the true picture into focus.*

The night was hot, the sea an unruffled inland lake so smooth you could find stars in it. He lay back in his deck chair looking shoreward at the mountain wall that was Mexico's west coast. Someone ran along the narrow deck and then she was down on her knees beside him, clinging to him, pressing her face against his chest.

'Oh, Red!' she cried.

His fingers touched her neck, moved up through the soft mass of her hair. 'Yes, Mumsie.'

'I'm afraid.'

'Of what?'

'You won't come back. You'll leave me in Los Angeles and you won't come back.'

'Of course I'll come back.'

'You mustn't. I'm no good. I'll never be any good. Such a black soul, darling.'

'Black velvet,' Red said. 'Anyway, I like black souls.'

'Right now you do. After a while you'll start thinking.'

'Who named you Mumsie?'

'A man.'

28

'Your father?'

'He called me Harriet. Don't ask about the other.'

'I want to ask. I like to pry into your past. It excites me.'

'Someday it won't. Someday you'll start seeing ghosts. Oh, Red, I've a secret for you.'

'Say it.'

'I adore you.'

He found her lips and then the dream began.

In the night it rained and he heard the rain hitting the deck. Suddenly the tiny cabin was cool. Mumsie asked: 'Who wrote it?'

'Wrote what?'

'You know what. The poem I'm thinking.'

'I'm not a mind reader,' Red said sleepily. 'How do I know the poem you're thinking?'

'It goes, "When I am dead and over me bright April shakes down her rain-drenched hair." '

'Go back to sleep and stop being so cheerful,' Red said. He turned over away from her and lay there looking at the gray patch that was the window, listening to the rain drop down, listening to the thump of the engines and the slap of the waves against the rusty steel.

'Teasdale,' Mumsie said. 'That's who wrote it.'

She put her body tight against his back and he could feel her warm breath on his neck. 'I wouldn't like it. I wouldn't like being dead and having April let her rain-drenched hair down on me. Would you like it, Red?'

'Go to sleep.'

'I wouldn't have you with me. That's why I wouldn't like it.'

He turned and held her close. 'How did you happen to read Sarah Teasdale?'

'A man read it to me.'

'The same man who named you Mumsie?'

'No.'

'My God!' Red said. 'What do you do — collect men?'

'I told you not to pry. Anyway, they don't matter any more.'

29

'That's heartening.'

'Do I ask you about all your women?'

'Want to hear?'

'No.'

'Tell me about Whit Sterling.'

'No.'

'He read you the Teasdale poem.'

'Yes. How did you know?'

'The only time I saw him, a guy was reading *North of Boston* aloud to him. He was in bed with a stomach ache. When you get through with me, will you shoot me?'

'Red!' The name was a crying protest.

'I just wanted to make sure,' Red said. 'Now let's go to sleep.'

'Haven't we anything better to do?'

'Yes,' Red said.


He took bits of her life and put them together – bits whispered to him in the night. Yet there were not enough to round it out. So he made up the rest. He had time enough on that trip up the coast. The old ship didn't seem to give a damn if it ever rounded the San Pedro breakwater. Nor did he.

An unpleasant job confronted him – leaving Mumsie, heading east and trying to make Whit Sterling swallow a tall tale. Not that he worried much about it. He was too busy finding a soul for Mumsie to worry about anything. Yet, when they left the ship and rode by taxi into the hot, dispirited mediocrity that was Los Angeles he decided to put it off for a while.

There was a little house in Laurel Canyon with a creek in front of it. A footbridge crossed the creek and sometimes, when the boys at the reservoir opened the gates, water ran under the bridge. It was cool and quiet in the canyon. Behind the house a hill rose steeply. You could walk up the creek and then there were no houses – nothing but brown hills on which the Yucca candles were burning out. At night the coyotes howled on the ridge. Mumsie said she used to hate them. That was because they made her lonely. Mumsie said she had forgotten what loneliness was so she didn't hate them anymore.

A week, and then Red started worrying. So she drove him to Pasadena in the car they had bought and cried a little while they waited for the train.

'I wish you wouldn't go,' Mumsie said.

'I have to,' Red said.

'Why?'

'I'm running out of money,' Red told her. 'I want to sell my business to my partner and start another here. And I can't do it unless I settle up with Sterling.'

Mumsie's eyes grew thoughtful. She started to speak. Watching her, he felt a sudden sharp distrust. Perhaps – He wouldn't finish the thought. Her speech went unsaid.

He kissed her and swung up on the steps as the train started moving. Seeing her so small and alone in the fading sunlight, his faith came back.

# CHAPTER FOUR

*The last car pulled out of the driveway. Out in the hall there was
the mumble of tired voices as Guy Parker's boys trekked off to bed.
Red rolled over on his back, found a cigarette, lighted it and
watched the smoke spiral toward the ceiling. Now Mumsie was
Guy's woman. For how long? When she got tired of him would
she put a bullet in his stomach? Or give him a sack to hold and
walk out on him. That would give Guy and Red something in
common, Red thought wryly. He had been left holding the sack. It
was still in his hands.*

HE MET GUY two weeks after he came back from New York
with ten thousand dollars of Jack Fisher's money in his
pocket. Jack had jumped at the chance to buy him out and
Jack hadn't asked questions. Neither had Whit Sterling.

'So you couldn't find her,' Sterling had said coldly. 'All
right. Run along. When I need you again I'll look you up.'

That was all there was to it. Either Red's reputation for
truth satisfied Whit or he had lost interest in Mumsie.

Red's office had been opened a week when Guy walked
in one morning, his gold chief's badge gleaming, his blue
uniform so well tailored you hardly thought of him as a
copper.

Guy's hand was thin and hard. 'Glad to have you around,'
he said. 'It's going to seem odd having an honest private eye
working the town.'

Red gave him a cigar and waited without comment.

32

A police chief didn't ordinarily drop around to hand out compliments.

'Heard a lot about you,' Guy said. 'All good.'

'That's fine.'

'Lined up anything?'

'Nothing big.'

Guy chewed on the unlighted cigar for a while. He said suddenly, 'Goddamn it, I've got to trust you.'

There was no answer to that. Red looked through the window at the garish decorations on the dance hall on the other side of the street.

'I got a kid,' Guy said. 'He's in a jam and I can't do anything about it. Some guy's bleeding him. I want you to find out who and why.'

'What about your boys?'

Guy laughed. 'Tell them? Christ. Let a cop in on family secrets? I'd be out in the street. You know how this town is. Full of longhairs just waiting to needle you. Full of guys waiting to help them.'

Business in a new town would be lean unless he had someone to give him a hand. Across the desk was a thin guy who was in a position to throw a lot of cases his way. 'I'll take a whirl at it,' Red said.

Red didn't see Guy again for a couple of weeks. One night the police chief came across the footbridge and rapped on the door. He handed Red a bundle of dough and said if there was ever anything he could do, just ask. Mumsie was reading in the chair across the room and Guy looked at her through the open door. He said maybe he could stop long enough for a quick one. He stayed for five quick ones and most of the time he gave his attention to Mumsie.

'He has a yen,' Red said when Parker went away.

'I don't want it.' Mumsie came over and sat in his lap. 'I only want your yens.'

'It might be fun sleeping with a cop.'

'You've an evil mind.'

'What's evil about sleeping with cops? They're limbs of the law. They're whited sepulchers.'

'Not that one. Don't talk about him any more. Tell me a secret, darling.'

'I adore you,' Red whispered, and he meant it.

He kept on meaning it through the coldest winter the town had ever known and the wettest spring that followed. Then Jack Fisher showed up to bring his world down around his ears.

The cabin they found on Pyramid Creek, just off the American River road from Lake Tahoe to Placerville, belonged to the man who owned the store at Strawberry. It stood back from the creek a way and the bedroom windows looked up toward Horsetail Falls. At night you could hear the water pouring down the rocks.

A clump of lodgepole pine grew in front of the cabin. If you cut into the bark it smelled like apples. Down the hill was the highway but you couldn't see it and you couldn't see the river. But you could see the gorge through which the river ran and you could see the snow-covered peaks off to the right. When the sun dropped low enough the peaks were red for a little while.

They rented the cabin late in the afternoon and bought a lot of canned stuff and put it in the kitchen and cooked supper. They worked together, stopping now and then to look through the window at the dusk filling the canyon. After supper they took a cot out on the porch and lay on it, listening to the creek, with the husk of an old moon looking at them and the ghosts of a million lost worlds.

'We should have come here right away,' Mumsie said. 'We never should have gone to Los Angeles.' She pressed close to him.

'He didn't see you,' Red said. 'Anyway, he's probably forgotten all about you.'

'He saw you and he doesn't forget.'

'That dame who was with him won't let him remember

34

his past,' Red said. 'A year is a long time. And he wasn't in Los Angeles looking for you. He was opening a dog track.'

'Then why did we run?'

'I don't like Southern California.'

'Even with me around?'

'Even with you around.'

'What do we do next?'

'We stay here until snow flies,' Red said. 'Then we'll go to Reno and I'll open an office and we'll live on the fat of the land.'

'Like we did in Los Angeles?' Mumsie asked skeptically.

'Los Angeles is no place for a detective. Too much competition from the cops.'

'You're not telling the truth,' Mumsie said. 'You wouldn't have left in such a hurry if you weren't afraid.'

'I'm not afraid of Sterling,' Red said. That was true enough. Meeting the man in front of the Biltmore Hotel hadn't worried him at all. Sterling had expressed surprise at seeing him. They had exchanged pleasantries, then Whit and his blonde friend had climbed into a waiting Cadillac and had driven away. What worried – or rather annoyed – him was a visitor he had had at five o'clock one evening a few days before. Red's secretary had gone home and Red was alone in the dingy office on the fourth floor of an old building at Fifth and Main streets. He heard footsteps crossing the outer office. His door opened and Jack Fisher stood in the doorway.

'Surprise,' Jack Fisher said. He entered, closed the door behind him and stood there grinning at Red. 'Aren't you pleased to see your ex-partner, old boy?'

Red got up, came around the desk and they shook hands. 'What brings you out here?'

'This and that.'

'How's Gertrude?'

Fisher dismissed her with a shrug. 'Gone the way of all flesh.'

'Working?'

35

'Sort of.'

'How's the racket?'

'Good.' Fisher looked around him at the tired furniture and the dirty windows. 'This is funny.'

'What?'

'Finding you in a dump. Did you spend it all?'

'The ten grand you paid me is tucked safely away, Jackson. I'm living on earnings.

'I wasn't talking about the ten grand.'

'No?'

'I was talking about a whole lot more. Say fifty-six grand.'

'Sit down,' said Red, 'and stop talking nonsense.'

Fisher sat. He took out a cigar, lighted it and grinned at Red through the fragrant smoke. 'Whit swallowed that crap,' he said, 'because he doesn't know you like I do.'

'You working for Whit?'

'Nope. But I could be.'

'Why don't you, then?'

'I can make more dough keeping my trap shut.'

'I doubt it.'

'He'd be mighty surprised to know you had an office here.'

'He knows it. I saw him today.'

'But he doesn't know about Mumsie.'

Fisher's grin widened. He flicked ashes on the worn carpet, waiting for a reply that wasn't forth-coming. 'He doesn't know you two are living in a house in Laurel Canyon, old boy. Shall I give him your phone number?'

'You shouldn't waste that talent on me,' Red said. 'You should save it for your clients.'

'Always the card,' Fisher grinned. 'Covering up with a quip. How about it?'

'Run along.' Red locked his desk and stood up. Fisher also stood up.

'Tomorrow night.' Fisher's face lost its pleasant look. 'That's the deadline.'

'Sorry to disappoint you, Jackson. Mumsie spent all the dough she took.'

36

Fisher made a gesture of disbelief. 'She tell you that?'

Red opened the door, motioned Fisher out.

'Either you're a liar or just a plain goddamned fool,' said Fisher as he passed Red. He threw a sneer over one shoulder, pitched the half-smoked cigar short of the wastebasket and crossed the room.

'Go home and read some more fairy tales. I'll see you tomorrow-night.'

The door closed. Red went over and picked up the cigar butt, made sure it was out and dropped it in the wastebasket. Then he picked up the phone and dialed a number.

'Start packing, my darling,' Red said when Mumsie answered. 'We're going fishing.'

The moon slid out of sight behind the trees. Red lay beside Mumsie and thought about Fisher and what Fisher had said. Presently he asked, 'Did you tell the truth, darling?'

'About what?' Her voice was sleepy.

'The money you took from Sterling.'

She pulled away from him and sat up. 'I'm going to bed.'

His hand held her. 'Did you, Mumsie?'

'That does it.' Her fingers were gentle as she took his hand away. 'You talked to him again and now you're wondering who told the truth. You'll keep on wondering. So it won't work any more.'

He wished he could see her face. He wished he could see the expression in her eyes, but the stars gave only enough light to tell him she was standing there above him.

'It's been nice,' Mumsie said.

He got up, slid one arm around her. 'I'm curious, that's all. I don't give a damn how much you stole from him. I've plenty left and I can work. But I don't want you laughing at me. I don't want you saying, "What a sucker he is – what a poor goddamned sucker!"'

'Stop it!' she cried out at him.

His arm tightened. 'Why are you so afraid of Whit, Mumsie?'

'I'm not.'

'Sit down.' He forced her back on the cot. Still holding her he told her about Jack Fisher.

Mumsie listened and she seemed to be hunting for lost stars. She said, after a while, 'I don't blame you for doubting, Red. I don't blame you a bit. You know too much about me. It doesn't do to know too much.'

'I'll stop doubting,' Red whispered. Yet he knew he never would.

Mr. Fisher put in an appearance two days later. Red wasn't surprised to see him because Red had confided in his secretary where he was going. Jack had a way with secretaries – he should have remembered that.

'Nice country,' Fisher said, looking up the canyon toward the falls. 'Wouldn't mind staying here myself.' He glanced at Mumsie and added, 'under the circumstances.'

'Stick around,' Red told him. 'There's an extra room.'

Fisher pushed past Red into the cabin. He leaned against the table and looked at Mumsie. 'Where's the money?'

'She didn't take it,' Red protested, trying to make the protest convincing.

'That's what she says. She's a dirty, lying little bitch.'

Red hit him. Off balance Fisher fell back over the table, lay on the rough boards cursing them both. Painfully he pulled himself up. Red hit at him again. This time Fisher ducked and went for his gun. Red kept on coming. Fisher backed up against the wall and his little eyes were black with fear. He licked his fat lips and pointed the gun at Red. Suddenly they were fighting for the gun. When Fisher pulled the trigger the muzzle was aimed the wrong way.

Mumsie wouldn't stay in the cabin with Fisher's body. They went down by the creek and waited for dark and now there was a wall between them. It would be all right, he kept telling himself, because he wanted it to be, because he didn't want to lose her, because he wanted to stay blind. When you create something, you hate to see it dissolve into nothingness.

38

They'd move on together and the doubt would go and they'd forget Jack Fisher. That wouldn't be too hard to do.

The canyon filled with darkness. East, the sunlight faded from the range and soon the trees stood out no longer. Soon they were vague shadows on the darkening hills.

Red kissed her. 'I won't be long.' He climbed the path to the cabin.

As he bent to pick up Fisher's body, a thought occurred to him. In the bedroom he found Mumsie's purse and tucked in a pocket of the purse was an account book on a Los Angeles Savings bank. He lighted a match and by its feeble flame looked at the figures in the book and then he knew. Mumsie had deposited fifty-one thousand dollars in the bank. All over. The dream ended.

There was a little meadow just off the creek up near the falls and he carried Jack Fisher's body there and put it on the grass. Then he started digging a grave.

He had stopped to rest when he heard, above the murmur of the creek, the sound of a car starting. Lights swung away from the cabin and down the road to the highway. He watched them disappear. He went back to his digging, not angry with her, not angry with himself for being such a fool.

He'd get over it, he knew. He'd be lonely for a while, lonely for a myth. And Mumsie? With that wad of money she should be very happy. Money was something you could hold and count. Love? Hell, you could pick that up in a Mexican cafe when you needed it.

*The sound of Guy's voice awakened him. Red sat up and rubbed his rough jaw.*

*'Feel better?' Guy asked.*

*'Fine,' Red said.*

*Guy came over and sat on the bed. 'Here's the setup. There's a girl who works for this Eels. She's okay. You see her first –'*

# CHAPTER FIVE

AT NOON, Jimmy Caldwell, the game warden, left his office and walked briskly up the street toward the Miller Realty Company. It was a fine clear day, warm without being hot, the sort of a day that made you forget Bridgeport didn't have the finest climate in the world, that there were weeks on end when snow blanketed the great meadow. In front of the hardware store Caldwell stopped for a minute to look at the display of fishing poles. Automatically his right hand moved in the gesture of a fly fisherman and that brought Ellis Gore, the owner, out.

'Hello, Jim,' Ellis said. 'When did you get back?'

'Last night.'

'How was L.A.?'

'Same as ever.'

'Hear you bought the Carlisle place. That right?'

Caldwell nodded. 'Yep.'

'Nice place. Going to move out there?'

'I don't know yet,' Caldwell said.

Ellis winked at him. 'Depends on things, huh?'

'Yes, sir,' Caldwell said.

'Red Bailey's out of town,' Ellis spoke casually, not looking at the bulky figure in the green uniform.

'I heard that.' Caldwell moved on up the street. Ellis looked after him, grinned and went back inside.

The game warden glanced at his wrist watch, started moving faster. Some men on the hotel steps called to him.

He returned their greeting but didn't stop. He knew well enough they wanted him to so they could tell him Bailey was out of town. The thought filled him with anger. That redheaded son of a bitch! That ugly, worn-out bastard! Someday he was going to kick the guy's teeth in. If he kept on hanging around Ann, by God, he certainly would kick his teeth in. He transferred his anger momentarily to Ann Miller. She should have better sense. Running after the guy like a high school kid – chasing him all over the goddamned place. And him old enough to be her father, almost.

He throttled his emotions because he was in front of the white, one-story building that housed the Miller Realty Company and he could see Ann through the open door. She sat at her desk, banging away at a typewriter, her dark head bent a little. Jesus, she's pretty, Caldwell thought. The love he had for her almost choked him. He felt his face getting red.

Trying to be casual he sauntered in and stood there flicking dust off one coat sleeve. Ann looked up, gave him a small smile, went on with her work.

'You're looking pretty sharp,' Caldwell said.

'Am I?' She typed another line, pulled the paper from the machine, ran her gaze over the typed script.

'Little thin.' Caldwell picked the paper knife off her desk and pretended he was a knife thrower. 'Looks like you could use some nourishment. Maybe some lunch.'

'Be with you in a minute,' Ann said. She left her desk and went into her father's office. Caldwell followed, grinned at the paunchy gray man with a pencil behind one ear. Canby Miller, forgetting his stomach was bothering him, said cordially, 'The boy himself. Hi there, Jimmy. Why ain't you out there rousting campers around?'

'Nobody's going to break the law for quite a while – unless they use dynamite.' Caldwell leaned against the door frame and some of his self-confidence came back. Anyway, Canby liked him a lot. That gave him at least one strike on Bailey because Ann thought much of her father and mother and did just about what they told her. Like working here in Bridgeport when what she had wanted was to go to Reno or L.A. or New York.

Miller scrawled his name at the bottom of the letter Ann had given him, then started reading it through.

'Come on,' Caldwell said. 'Hurry it up, you old slave driver. Let the girl get her lunch.'

'Didn't you want to see me?' Miller spread fake disappointment over the words.

'What for? Why, all you do is try to sell a man insurance he don't need or some broken-down piece of land an Okie wouldn't want.

'And what do you do?' Miller sneered genially. 'Pick up poor unfortunates who haven't got two bucks for a fishing license. Look at that badge. You haven't polished it for a month.'

'That's so it won't scare people.' Caldwell felt better now. Yes, sir, Candy liked him, wanted him for a son-in-law. That was swell. Canby was one swell guy.

'When you going to start working,' Miller asked, 'and stop running around playing fly cop?'

'When you stop robbing widows.'

Miller patted his stomach, grew serious. 'Well, we put it over.'

'We sure did.'

'A real steal,' Miller said proudly. 'That fool didn't take the trouble to find out what land was worth around here. When you going to move out?'

'Couple of weeks.'

'You sure got a real buy. You can thank Canby Miller for that, son. Maybe Canby isn't the best operator around California but he'll do until a better one comes along.'

'Someday you're going to break your right arm patting your own back that way. Come on, Ann, I'm hungry.' Caldwell stood aside for her, his round, pale blue eyes trying to tell her how much he loved her. She was sure pretty, and every day she got prettier. Desire for her came up into his

42

throat and choked him. He took a deep breath and followed her out. On the sidewalk he took her arm possessively, straightened his shoulders and guided her across the street toward the Acme Home Cafe. She was his and no ugly, red-haired bastard was going to mess things up.

Ann sensed what he was thinking. She threw a sober, fleeting glance up at his round, tanned face. Poor Jimmy, she thought. Poor, good, dependable Jimmy. Such a nice, solid, unimaginative boy. But that was the trouble. He was too solid, too nice.

A couple waved at them from a pick-up rattling down the street. They waved back. Caldwell smiled down at her.

'What a day!' He pulled the thin, cool air into his lungs. 'Boy! How's about taking a run out to my new joint after lunch?'

She started to refuse but changed her mind. 'All right.'

'It's a pip,' Caldwell said. 'Wait till I tell you what I'm going to do with it.'

The old Carlisle place had been there since 1880, but the man who built it had known what he was doing. In this neck of the woods you built for keeps, using redwood and heavy timbers, pitching your roofs so the snow would slide off, planting rows of trees to break the force of the icy winds that swept across the level plateau all winter long. The house was a big one badly in need of paint, but not a shingle was loose, not a board out of place. The porch was just as solid as it had been sixty years ago, the floors as sound. Caldwell stopped on the top step and stared proudly around him. Five hundred level acres, crisscrossed by little creeks. A great warm barn. He saw it not as it was – shabby, paintless, the fences down in places, the corrals broken, the fields empty of cattle and sheep – but as it would be a year hence. White-faced cattle sleeping in the sun. Great balls of white wool that were fat sheep nibbling the thick meadow grass. The two-story house white and shining on the hill. The barn bulging with hay. He'd put a silo over there – a cement one. Green lawn would slope down to the road. Over there by the cottonwoods,

43

maybe a swimming pool. A pool with a couple of dressing rooms near the edge and maybe a paved court and a barbecue pit. A really swell layout. He looked down at Ann on the step below him. A good, strong, slim girl in a white linen dress – just the sort of wife a man needed.

'Boy!' Caldwell said. Ann threw a smile up at him. He found a key in a pocket, went to the front door and opened it, stood aside with a courtly bow. 'Enter, madame.' Ann brushed past him.

The house smelled of mold and dust. The air was cold and dead for the doors and windows hadn't been opened since old Mrs. Carlisle died a year ago. Nothing had been touched. The sitting room was just as she had left it – the furniture standing around stiffly in the dim, high-ceilinged room, the flowered carpet almost as bright as the day it was bought. And why not? No one had used the sitting room. This was the first time Jim Caldwell had been in it. The only room he had seen was the kitchen. That was a long time ago when he was a kid and used to bring Mrs. Carlisle's groceries up from town.

'We'll open her up,' Caldwell said. 'Put a big window there so you can look out over the valley. Tear that little bitty fireplace out and put one in a man can get warm by.'

'That will be fine,' Ann said, her voice impersonal.

We? Not me, she thought, and then she was very sorry for him. Poor old Jimmy!

They went into the big kitchen where the huge wood stove took up almost one wall. Caldwell explained how they were going to put in a sink and electric lights and a big window over the sink so you could see what was going on in the world when you washed dishes.

'A fireplace too,' Caldwell said. 'I've always wanted me a fireplace in the kitchen ever since I was a kid.'

Despite herself Ann began entering into the spirit of the thing. They discussed curtains. They discussed light fixtures. They went upstairs and figured out where the bathrooms should be. No need to touch the bedrooms. They were swell

– great big rooms with plenty of windows and you wouldn't have to get new furniture. Just new mattresses and pillows and curtains and stuff like that because the bird's-eye maple fitted the rooms. Maybe some bright pictures like they had in early American houses in the *American Home* magazine.

A porch ran across the side of the house upstairs.

'We'll screen her,' Caldwell said. 'A swell place for kids to sleep in the summer. Screen her and fix some good heavy shutters to put up in the winter. Boy, I'll bet you could sleep out here all year, once you got used to it!' He looked down into the yard. 'Over there a swimming pool,' he pointed. 'Won't that be something! String lights up and have parties at night. We'll get us a Delco system, or maybe dam up the crick and put a wheel in. Can't do it all at once though.' He slid one arm around her. 'Jeez, Ann!' he said in a choked voice. 'Jeez, I love you!'

She was going to tell him she didn't love him. She was going to say, 'Jimmy, I love him so very much I can't live without him. I lie awake most of the night thinking how much I love him.' But she said nothing. She stood there on the upstairs porch of the old Carlisle place that was now the Caldwell ranch and looked across the great meadow at the towering Sierras. A quail whistled in the meadow. A hawk slid down the sky.

'I must go back,' she said, not looking at his eager, loving eyes.

Caldwell sighed. 'That's right.'

They went downstairs and out. He locked the door, followed her across the yard, stopping once to look proudly at his house. He must be careful when they painted not to hurt the rosebush. That was one thing he wouldn't change, that rosebush climbing up the porch. He wanted to yell, he was so happy. Like a young stallion he ran after Ann, opened the door for her and lifted her in, then ran around and jumped under the wheel of his station wagon. As he drove away he whistled. But he stopped whistling when they hit the outskirts of town. Red Bailey's service station crouched

45

by the highway and Ann asked him to stop for a minute. The Kid came over to the car, grinning.

'Hello, Kid. Is he back?'

The Kid shook his head, took a pencil and note pad from his shirt pocket and scribbled on the pad:

'Got a letter. He won't be back for two weeks. He's in New York.'

Seeing the hurt in her eyes as she read the note the Kid took the pad back and wrote: 'He wrote you too, he said.'

Ann read what he had written. 'Thanks, Kid.' With nervous fingers she found her cigarettes, gave him one, lighted one for herself. She put one hand on his arm, squeezed it.

'So he run out on you,' Caldwell said angrily.

'Shut up!' Ann said in a cold little voice. 'Shut up, you stupid –' She let the sentence trail off.

Caldwell drove, staring at the road, not seeing the people in front of the stores, not seeing anything, thinking, Oh that dirty, big bastard! That stinking, ugly, red son of a bitch! Will I fix him!

In front of the realty office, he jammed on the brakes and opend the door for her. Ann turned to him.

'I'm sorry, Jim,' Ann said.

'Okay,' Caldwell said. 'You're sorry. Okay, okay.'

He slammed the door and drove away.

# CHAPTER SIX

SOME KIDS on roller skates were playing hockey in the street. They skated back and forth, whanging a chunk of asphalt with sticks whittled out of pieces of old lumber. If a car came along to break up the game momentarily, they told the driver what they thought of him. It was a dreary neighborhood. There were a couple of halfway decent apartment houses in the block but the rest were dirty brick structures, jammed close together. People sat on the fire escapes or on the stoops, trying to get cool. The East River was two blocks away but that didn't help any because there wasn't any breeze. Nobody paid any attention to the hockey players, even when they slammed each other across the shins.

When Red's cab appeared, crawling through the hot dusk, two boys were trying to murder each other in the middle of the street. The cab driver put his hand on the horn button and headed straight for them, so the boys stopped fighting and gave him their attention. They jumped on the running board and stuck their heads through the windows.

'You bastid,' one of the kids said. 'You dirty bastid! Who do you think you're running down?'

'Go on,' the driver said, giving the kid a shove.

Something banged into the rear of the cab. The driver put on the brakes and opened the door. He grabbed the nearest kid, took his stick away from him and let him have one across the backside. 'Who done that?' he demanded.

Red sat forward, grinning. New York, he decided, hadn't

changed much. It was just as dirty and just as hot. The kids were as tough as ever and the cab drivers had the same curious disinterest in staying alive or letting anyone else stay alive.

'I done it,' a thin voice yelled. A piece of asphalt rocketed past the cab driver's head. The driver hurled the stick at his assailant, got in the car and started moving. Red looked back. The kids yelled curses after them, then went on with their game.

'Nice kids,' the driver said.

'It's the heat,' Red said. 'Makes them irritable. They don't get their afternoon naps.'

'You ain't kiddin',' the driver said. 'Naps.' He made a sound that might have been laughter and pulled the cab over to the curb in front of a remodeled tenement. Red gave him a dollar and got out.

'Want me to wait?'

Red shook his head. There was a garbage can at the right of the entrance and someone had kicked it over. The sight of it made him wonder why anyone lived in New York. He found Meta Carson's name on the directory by the door and put a finger on the bell. He turned to watch the cab pull away. Down the street the kids were yelling as they played. It occurred to him that the sound wasn't at all sad. In other places when you heard children's voices in the dusk it filled you with loneliness, but not in New York. The lock gave off a buzz like an angry rattlesnake. He opened the door and went in.

The hallway was dark and fairly cool. He went along to the back and heard a voice say, 'Come in.' He found himself in a big room that opened out on a small courtyard. A high brick wall surrounded the yard and at the back was what looked like a church.

The occupant of the apartment was a tall blonde girl of twenty-eight. She wore slacks and a blue silk blouse. Apparently there was nothing under the blouse but Meta Carson.

She said, 'Sit down and I'll get you a drink. I hope you like gin and tonic.'

A picture of a Negro woman nursing a baby hung on the wall back of the couch. Red didn't like it. He sat down and watched the blonde. She opened a couple of doors at the other end of the room, revealing an icebox, a stove and a sink. 'This your first trip to New York?' she asked, mixing the drinks without the aid of a jigger.

'I was born here,' Red said.

'How did they happen to ring you in on this?'

'I was handy. And you?'

'I was handy too.' She put the glasses on the coffee table and sat down. Her legs were inordinately long, her feet bare.

'Parker said you worked for Eels.'

'I'm his secretary.'

'That's cozy,' Red said and sipped his drink. It was very cold. 'Where do you fit in this mess?'

'Here and there.' She didn't look at him. 'What did Parker tell you?'

'To phone you. I did and here I am.'

A package of Kools was on the table. She put one in a holder and Red lit a match. His hand was not too steady and she caught his wrist in her fingers and held the flame to the cigarette. Her fingers were cold. 'Tomorrow night you meet Eels. I'm going up there for a moment before dinner. You go along and look around.'

'And then?'

'He'll take some stuff home with him in a few days. When he does I'll tell you and get you in. He won't be there. He'll be with me.'

'As simple as that,' Red said dryly. 'They haul a man across a continent to play burglar.'

She watched him through the smoke, her head tilted a little. He didn't like the expression in her eyes. He was puzzled and not a little wary. The whole business smelled. You couldn't put things together – Parker and Eels and Meta

49

Carson. But what could you do about it but string along and hope to Christ you weren't being handed a hot one?

'You've nothing to worry about,' Meta said.

'I'm glad of that.'

'Another drink?'

'I'll buy you one if you don't mind walking. My favorite bar is up the street a bit.'

'You'll have to wait while I change.'

'Put on shoes,' Red said. 'Otherwise you're fine.'

'You don't wear slacks to bars, Mr. Bailey.' She rose and disappeared through a door in the hall.

There were some bits of ice at the bottom of his glass, and he filled his mouth with them. He wondered if Meta was as cold as she seemed. Women with figures as good as she had weren't usually. Maybe she was repressed. Maybe she had something on her mind. He got up presently and went through the screen doors into the small court that had enough potted plants standing around to be called a garden. In the apartment above, a woman with a thin, hard voice was telling somebody off. Higher up a radio was giving forth with bad music. It was dark now and he managed to find a few stars in the murky patch of sky.

Meta's voice made him turn. She was standing just inside the door. She wore a rust-colored gabardine suit and an oddly shaped hat that was probably very smart. 'Did you find the sky?' She didn't wait for an answer. 'But of course. You're a detective.'

Walking through the hot night, he changed his mind about Meta Carson. She moved along close to him, one shoulder touching his arm now and then, her voice bright and warm. She had fire in her, all right. Or maybe she was trying to keep his mind occupied, maybe she didn't want him to figure things out. The hockey players had departed, but Forty-Eighth Street wasn't quiet. Women yelled at each other across the narrow way or screamed for their offspring. The offspring paid little heed. Two girls traded witticisms with a man in a delivery truck. A crap game was in progress on the

50

sidewalk in front of a small grocery. The woman who ran the place stood in the door watching the boys roll the cubes against a brick wall.

'I'm not hungry yet,' Meta said. 'Let's look at the river.'

They crossed First Avenue, went past a row of garages and under the new East River Drive. A barge loaded with pilings was tied at a pier and the air had the good, sharp smell of fresh creosote. Some kids played on the barge.

The path went along the bank and widened. A few little trees struggled against the fence. On the benches people sat staring at the dark water, waiting patiently for a breeze that refused to accommodate them. Most of the people were silent. Ahead was the bridge, a few cars crawling across it. Red and Meta found a vacant bench and sat down.

'I come here nearly every night,' Meta said. 'I love the river.'

Red said he did too. But he wasn't thinking about the river moving sluggishly along. He was wondering what in hell he was mixed up in. An ex-cop who ran a gambling joint in Reno and a New York attorney. A woman, with class written all over her, who was somehow tied in with Parker and who didn't hesitate to sell out the man she worked for. It wasn't good. It wasn't good at all. He wasn't coming out of this untouched. That was certain. For the first time in his life he felt helpless. Not afraid – because he couldn't find anything to be afraid of.

Meta started asking him questions. To keep him from asking himself questions probably. Was it exciting being a detective? Had he ever been shot at? Did he like New York? He found answers of a sort, gave them to her, all the while thinking, what the hell is this about? When are they going to give me the business? When and how and why?

A tug grunted by, pushing a couple of barges loaded with freight cars. Over Brooklyn a searchlight stabbed with its finger at a cloud, found what it was looking for and went out. Red stood up. He was tired of answering questions. He was tired of asking himself questions. What was going to happen would happen and that was that. When you came right down to it, it didn't matter much. It really didn't matter at all. Even if he was a worthy citizen full of good deeds and honors, it wouldn't matter.

# CHAPTER SEVEN

LLOYD EELS was a tall man who hadn't come off the assembly line. Somebody had found some spare parts lying around and had put them together carelessly, not bothering to get the bolts tight so that they seemed almost ready to come apart. He had black, sad eyes and a black mustache like an untrimmed hedge. No amount of combing would help his shock of hair. Red ordinarily didn't like attorneys. The ones he had known were either pompous and crooked or ratty and crooked. But he liked Eels.

The man was a bachelor and lived on Central Park South in an old apartment building that didn't belong among the newer and bigger structures. There was no doorman. Red punched the bell, announced himself and heard the click in the streetdoor lock. Across the hall from the superintendent's apartment was a small, automatic elevator that took him up to the fourth floor. They were remodeling one of the apartments on the floor and the hall was a mess of ladders, rolls of paper and buckets.

Eels opened the door for him and led him into the living room that opened on a balcony. Eels, by the looks of things, had plenty of money. He also had a decided yen for Meta Carson, who was sitting on the balcony with a Martini in her hand. Red wondered if he ever did anything about the yen. If so he was due for a surprise one of these days when he found out the lady had peculiar connections.

At first Eels was quiet, almost rude. Apparently he figured

Red was doing a bit of trepassing. But when he was told that Red came from California, that he was a distant relative of Meta's who didn't plan to stick around, Eels warmed up.

'I couldn't let Red leave town without meeting you.' Meta's voice dripped sweetness. 'Lloyd's my favorite boss,' she added, batting her eyes at Red. Eels almost purred.

'Meta seems to spend all her time thinking about you,' Red said. 'I'm beginning to understand her deep interest.'

Eels moved closer to Meta and put a gentle hand on her shoulder. 'You picked the wrong time to come to New York, Mr. Bailey. But at that, most any time is the wrong one. I never can understand why Californians come east.'

'Then you know California?'

'Very well. Particularly San Francisco.' He smiled at Red. 'There's a little restaurant on Pine Street I like tremendously.'

'Pierre's?'

'That's it.'

'I live in Bridgeport, near Reno,' Red said pointedly. 'Ever been to Reno?'

Meta shot a warning glance across at him.

'Once. It impressed me as tawdry. Cheap.'

'Wonderful country around it though,' Red evaded Meta's glance. 'Some fine ranches. A friend of mine has a beautiful place. Fellow named Parker.'

Eel's glance had only polite interest in it. Meta's voice didn't. 'He isn't interested in your friends, Red.'

'If he knew Parker, he'd be interested in him,' Red insisted. 'Quite a guy, Parker.'

Meta drained her glass and stood up. 'Red has people to see. We must be going.'

'No,' Eels protested. 'He just got here.'

'I'm in no hurry.' Red smiled at Meta.

'Stick around. We'll have dinner.' Eels trailed Meta through the terrace door.

'Can't,' Meta told him. 'Come on, Red.'

Eels threw a suspicious glance back at Red who moved

54

after them into the living room. Meta saw it. She took both Eel's hands and smiled up at him. 'Red's leaving tomorrow night. Then you'll have me all to yourself.'

Seeing the gratitude in Eels' eyes, Red became irritated. He wanted to hurl the girl over the balcony, stand there and watch her go spinning down. *The bitch*, he thought, *the dirty little bitch!* He wanted to start talking. He wanted to say, 'My lad, you're being screwed and I'm being screwed, and I've got a hunch you don't deserve it.' But would Eels listen? Probably not. When a man had it bad, there was no hope for him.

They might as well have stayed for another drink. Meta insisted on showing Red what a good amateur photographer Eels was, what fine books he had and what a beautiful apartment this was. Eels shambled around after them, watching Meta as though she was something lovely and precious and fine. That made Red feel pretty horrible, made him wish more than ever he knew what was going on.

'Sorry you have to go,' Eels said when they were finally at the door. 'Come again, won't you?'

'Thanks,' Red shook his outstretched hand.

Red stood aside to let Meta precede him through the door. Then because Eels obviously wanted a moment alone with the girl, he went into the hall and across to the elevator. He punched the button, heard the whir of machinery as the lift creaked into motion, heard Eel's low voice behind him.

'Tomorrow night, darling?'

'No, Lloyd.'

The cage climbed wearily up, stopped and the door slid open. Behind Red there was silence and he thought, hell, let the guy have his kiss or two while he still wants them because when he finds out about Meta Carson he won't want them any more. Then Eels spoke again.

'Goodnight, Meta.'

'Goodnight.'

'Monday morning?'

'Right.'

'The file's in order?'

'Yes.'

More silence. Meta crossed the hall and got into the elevator. She smiled past Red at the man waiting in the doorway.

'Goodbye,' Eels told them both.

'So long,' Red said and closed the door.

They didn't speak until they reached the street. It was cooler than it had been but not exactly pleasant. They walked down Sixth Avenue and turned south.

'You're a cute guy,' Meta said. 'But what did it get you?'

'I found out one thing. He doesn't know Parker.'

'Who said he did?'

'Parker said he had a friend Eels was pushing around. I didn't believe him.'

'So he has a friend.'

'Suppose I went back and spilled the little I know.'

'I wouldn't.'

'The guy's in love with you.'

'My dear boy,' Meta said. 'Of course he is. He's been making fumbles at me for six months.' She saw a cab down the block and went to it. Red opened the door and got in beside her.

'Graybar Building,' Meta told the driver. His name was Abe Cross and he was even meaner looking than the picture on his registration card.

'Gonna rain,' the driver said.

'That's right,' Red said.

The driver swung the cab around in the middle of the block.

Meta sat in the corner, smoking a Kool. Tonight she wore a white dress, simply cut. A white turban was trapped around her well-shaped head. She watched Red speculatively, a smile on her full lips. 'Can you find your way around the place?' she asked presently.

'Blindfolded. When do I play porch climber?'

'There's no hurry.'

'Fumbles,' Red said. 'That's an insulting way to speak of a guy. At least give him credit for a pass.'

'I'll be sorry when you leave. You could be good fun, Red.'

'I'm a card,' Red said. 'How long have you worked for him?'

'Six months.'

'What have they got on you?'

She tried to look surprised. 'Got on me?'

'Parker.'

'What could he have on me?'

'Plenty. Or you wouldn't be double-crossing such a nice guy.'

'Maybe I'm not double-crossing him. Maybe he's been pushing friends of mine around. You know how he makes his money?' Her tone had hardened.

'How?'

'He works for a guy, then digs up –' She thought better of it, shrugged.

'Digs up what?'

'Skip it. Has Parker got something on you?'

'A triffling little matter. Where are we going?'

'I'm getting out.' She spoke to the driver. 'Stop at the next intersection.'

'Okay lady,' the driver said.

'What about me?' Red asked.

'You'll find something to do.' The cab pulled up at the curb, she smiled at him and got out. Up the street a little way was the entrance to the Graybar Building.

'Now where?' the driver asked.

'St. Regis,' Red said. But the cab had gone only a half-block before he changed his mind. 'I'll get off here,' he told the driver, paid him, waited until the cab pulled away then headed back down the street. Meta was nowhere in sight.

In front of the Graybar Building he stopped and looked into the dimly lighted lobby. It was deserted. A thought occurred to him and he went inside and read the names on the directory. With no surprise he saw that Lloyd Eels occupied an office on the twelfth floor. Turning, he hurried out but stopped in a dark entryway nearby and waited.

The air was oppressive, heavy with the threat of rain and in the west thunder rumbled. A sailor and a thin, dark-haired girl sauntered by. When the sailor said something in a low voice the girl giggled and pressed against him. Out in the street the traffic flowed thinly. Five minutes. Ten, Fifteen. Whatever Meta Carson was up to took time – unless she hadn't gone into the building. Still he waited, standing in the shadowy entry, listening and watching. Then she came out walking briskly. In her right hand was a brief case. She crossed to the curb and stood there looking up and down the street. One hand went up as a cruising cab came slowly along. The cab swung around and stopped in front of her.

'Hudson River Club,' Meta said as she opened the door.

Watching the cab's tail-light disappear, Red considered visiting the Hudson River Club. He wanted very much to know what was in that brief case. But following her would be a waste of time, he decided, so he went instead to the St. Regis bar.

He had been sitting on a stool for two hours before he figured things out. Then it was too late. When he crawled along the balcony and peered into Eel's living room he realized that.

Lloyd Eels was sprawled on the floor and he was dead.

# CHAPTER EIGHT

A WIND HAD come up. It pushed the drapes aside and ran through the room, ruffling the dark hair of the man lying on the floor. Thunder rumbled somewhere but it was far away.

The body was the first thing Red saw when he made his way along the balcony from the vacant apartment next door. Getting into the building had been simple enough. He had shoved two or three buttons and someone had released the catch for him. The door into the apartment being redecorated was conveniently open. He had gone through it, out to the balcony and thence to Eels' place. He stood outside a moment, looking into the room. He went in and bent over the murdered man. Eels had been shot through the head.

Anger flared within him. The sons of bitches! Pulling something like this. Well, they weren't going to get away with it. He straightened, looked around him. On the wall at the left of the bookshelves a picture was pushed aside and a wall safe gaped open. Papers were scattered on the floor below it, the wind tumbling them about. He didn't pick them up or look through them. Hurriedly he moved around the room, trying to remember the things he had touched, wiping them clean with his handkerchief, knowing all the time that it was futile. Stupid. Jesus, he had been stupid! Falling for a set-up like this one. Well, he'd make it tough for them. And if they got him he wouldn't go alone. He'd take Parker, the Carson woman and anyone else who got in his way. But he mustn't lose his head. He had figured some of it out but only some of it. He needed time. And time was what he was going to have. Not much but maybe enough.

In the hall he found the linen closet, took from it a sheet and rolled Eels' body in the sheet. He opened the door into the hall and made sure no one was about. Then he lifted the sheet-wrapped body and carried it into the vacant apartment. The workmen had finished in the bedroom. That was the place. The bedroom closet. He located it and dumped his bundle on the floor. If luck was on his side they wouldn't find it for a while.

He straightened the body. Poor bastard, he thought. Poor unlucky bastard! He closed and locked the door, wiped the key clean and pushed it under the door.

Blood stained the rug where Eels had lain. Red rolled it up, shoved it behind the davenport and replaced it with the rug from the hall. Quickly he gathered the scattered papers, shoved them into the safe, closed it, spun the combination and wiped it clean. He put the picture back in place. No evidence of an intruder now. Anyone coming in to look for Eels would find everything in order. That's the way it must be.

He found the stairway, walked up two flights and pushed the elevator button. He was on his way down when the buzzer told him someone was waiting on the first floor. The stop button halted his descent. He thumbed number two hoping to God the car would obey him. It did and he got out, waited until the old cage climbed skyward again. Then he went down the stairs and out into the street.

Rain was falling. Rain drummed on the pavement and few people were about. He walked rapidly east, turned south at Fifth Avenue, his hat pulled low, the rain beating down on him, soaking through his light jacket, slopping into his shoes. He didn't mind. He was cool for the first time in two days.

He wanted a drink badly but knew there was no time. At Fifty-Fifth Street he got into a cab and told the driver to take him to Second Avenue and Forty-Seventh Street. From there he walked east until he was opposite Meta Carson's apartment building. A passageway led north alongside a church. He moved down the passage. A wall stopped him. He jumped, hooked his fingers on the top and pulled his lean body up. When he saw that her apartment was dark he dropped into the court. He stood close to the wall for a few moments, waiting. A party was in progress upstairs, the guests good and drunk. No one else was stirring.

Crouching he crossed to the double doors. Getting them open was a cinch. A passkey did the trick but he didn't go in right away. Carefully he wiped his shoes on the mat and wrung most of the water from his clothes. It was raining harder than ever and the thunder was right overhead. Lightning repeatedly slit the cloudbanks and the rain seemed to come down faster, as though it was pouring through the holes made by the ragged blades of light.

Inside be found the light switch and flipped it up. He began searching the place. Hs worked methodically and efficiently, leaving no evidence that anything had been disturbed. After a while he stopped long enough to pour some Scotch in a water glass. By the time he finished going through the place the glass was empty. The liquor served only to make him angrier than ever. He went back to Meta's desk for another look at its contents. It didn't help him much. Carson was a careful woman. He hunched over the desk, leaning on his elbows, his eyes half closed, knowing that in this room somewhere was part of the answer. But where? No letters, no addresses, nothing. He straightened suddenly. Someone was coming down the hall.

There was a door near the desk. It opened into a small closet and he had switched off the lights and was inside in one quick movement with the door closed. A key rattled in the lock. Footsteps crossed the room. A band of light grew under the door. He heard the sound of the telephone dial. Meta spoke:

'Sorry to bother you,' Meta's voice said. 'But I'm worried about Mr. Eels. He's home, I know. Yet he doesn't answer his phone.'

61

Silence followed. Someone at the other end apparently was speaking.

'I spoke to him not half an hour ago,' Meta said. 'I was to call him again. He said he'd wait there.' Again silence. Then the woman's low voice. 'Please do. Thanks.'

He heard her moving about the room. A cupboard opened. A glass clinked. She was pouring herself a drink. A good thing he put that bottle and glass away, he thought. The couch sighed as she sat on it. Presently the telephone bell shrilled and he heard her hurry to the desk.

'Yes?' her voice said. 'What's that? But – are you sure he isn't there?'

The person on the other end of the wire must have been very sure. 'You went all through the apartment? Well – thank you. I'm sorry I bothered you. But I was worried. Good night.'

The closet was small and very hot. Red downed his impulse to open the door. The thing to do was to wait. He pressed his face against the wall, listening. He heard her pacing nervously about, heard the clink of the glass. She must be puzzled, worried. She must be wondering what in hell had gone wrong. Perhaps she would light out for Eel's apartment presently. That would be fine. That would give him another shot at her apartment.

But she didn't go out. After a bit she came back to the desk and he heard the click of the telephone dial.

'Mr. Stefanos, please,' Meta said.

Red drew a deep breath and felt his nails bite into his palms.

Meta's fingers drummed impatiently on the desk top. She said something under her breath. Soon she spoke again into the phone. 'Thank you. Tell him to call Meta Carson right away.'

She was putting the receiver in its cradle when Red opened the door.

# CHAPTER NINE

LIGHTNING FLARED outside, filling the room with momentary brightness. The torn clouds spilled rain into the courtyard. Not until he stood beside her did Meta see him.

'Come on,' Red said. 'I want to talk.'

Meta didn't speak. Her lips parted and she put her hand over her mouth.

He led her to the couch and pushed her down. Her handbag was on the coffee table. He opened it and dumped its contents out. A small automatic clattered on the wood. He pocketed it and dropped on the couch beside her.

'We crossed you up, baby,' Red said.

'You sons of bitches!'

He flicked her mouth with his knuckles and then she was on him, clawing at him, slashing at his eyes with fingernails that were red daggers. His fingers dug into her right breast. She moaned and dropped her hands. Red relaxed his grip but kept one hand on her breast. 'Nice,' he said. She tried to pull her body away. 'Now talk.'

'No.'

Her breast was small in his cupped hand. Very gradually he squeezed the firm, warm flesh.

'Oh, God!' she moaned.

Red let her go, took a cigarette from the box on the table and lighted it. 'We've plenty of time.' He grinned at her, trying to look like a man who had all the time in the world, trying to hide the fact that he was listening for the sound of the buzzer that would announce Mr. Stefanos' arrival. 'Now tell me everything.'

'You're not Red Bailey.' Her voice was husky with fear.

Things were going better than he had hoped. He nodded. 'Right. I'm a ringer. So is the little guy. Mr. Eels was not as trusting as he seemed. He's heart-broken though. You've brought his world down around his ears. But he'll get over it. Disillusion is so much easier to take than death.'

'What are you going to do to me?'

'That depends.'

'On what?'

'Whether you cooperate.'

'And if I do?'

'Nothing happens to you. We're not concerned with you or your part in it. We want the big guy.' He crushed his cigarette in the crystal tray.

'Get me a drink.' Her hands were shaking now and she seemed to be having trouble with her breathing. She motioned toward the cupboard. Red rose, got the Scotch bottle and two glasses, spilled whisky in the glasses and sat down again.

She gulped greedily. Her voice was barely audible. 'You said – you said you were a ringer. And the little man. Where are the right ones?'

'In the can.'

'What do you want to know?'

'All of it. Let's begin with Red Bailey. He's a confused individual. Why was he picked for the patsy?'

'I don't know.' With a fingernail she traced the pattern of the couch cover and she didn't look at him. The shadows of her long lashes were like cob-webs on her pale skin. Again he reached for her breast. She pushed his hand away. 'That won't do any good. I don't know anything about Red Bailey.' She shot a suspicious glance at him. 'What are you so concerned about him for?'

Careful, Red told himself. He must tread lightly because the ice was very thin. 'We don't want to leave anything out

64

of the picture. All right. If you don't know about Bailey, we'll skip him. Let's talk about you.'

She hunted in the glass for courage, found it. 'I couldn't help it. I had to do what I was told.'

'Why?'

'It doesn't matter.'

With a wave of one hand, Red indicated she could skip that part. It was something he wanted very much to know but it would have to wait.

'I met Eels before I went to work for him,' Meta said. 'That's why I was picked for the job. He liked me. So I played up to him and then I said I needed work. So he put me in his office.' She stopped talking and wet her lips. Red hoped her mind was as dull as her eyes. He poured more whisky in the glasses and tried to act like a man who was doing a routine job. 'Go on,' he urged. 'We haven't all night.'

'Last week I was told what to do,' she explained. Red wanted to stop her there. He wanted to ask who told her but he didn't dare. 'Two men were coming to New York. One was named Bailey and the other Stefanos. I was to take Bailey to Eels' apartment, make sure he left his fingerprints around. I was to put something in Eels safe at the office.'

'What?'

'An affidavit made by a woman named McGonigle. It said that Bailey killed his partner in California ten years ago. It told where they could find the body.'

Red let the Scotch trickle down his throat, felt the warmth of it in his stomach. A good, complete job. No loose ends. Nothing left to chance. When Parker framed you they could hang you in the Metropolitan. A nice, heavy gold frame. That was Parker's police training.

'We'll find it in Eels' safe?'

'Yes. I put it there tonight.'

'No wonder Mr. Bailey was so upset,' Red said. 'What was your next step?'

'That was all. The rest was up to Stefanos.'

'You knew he was going to kill Eels?'

65

She emptied her glass rather than answer. He wondered if she had a conscience, if she knew what shame was. He said, 'Jesus, what a cold-blooded bitch!'

'I'm not going to talk any more.'

'Oh yes,' Red said. 'You haven't finished. What did you take out of Eels' office tonight?'

She hid her eyes behind heavy lids, put her glass down and dropped her hands in her lap. They were very small and white.

'I was waiting outside the Graybar Building,' Red said. 'You went in empty-handed. You came out with a brief case. What was in it?'

She looked up. 'What do you suppose?'

'The file on the case Eels was working on?'

'Of course.' Her eyes studied his face and now there was wariness in her expression.

The ice was thinner than ever.

'What did you do with the brief case?' Red leaned forward, trying to hide his nervousness behind the glass in his hand.

'Gave it to a guy.'

'Who?'

'Do you have to ask?' Her wary glance probed the face hidden by the highball glass.

'I want to be sure.'

'Go ask him for it then.'

'I plan to.' He couldn't sit here all night beating around the bush – he knew that. Stefanos would be along presently. Stefanos would stop by to make sure things were going on schedule. And Red didn't want to be there when that happened. Nor did he want Meta to know he was Red Bailey just yet. Might as well shove off because she was wising up fast. He got slowly to his feet. 'I could take you in tonight. I'm not going to. I'm going to give you a few hours to think things over.' He headed for the door, stopped with his hand on the knob and looked back. She was staring after him, frowning.

66

'Good night,' Red said. 'And good luck. You'll need it, baby.' He grinned and let himself into the hall.

The rain had stopped. The wind was sweeping the clouds south, not being very thorough about it. The worn-out moon struggled wearily across the untidy sky and its anemic light fell like dust on the city. Red came out, looked cautiously up and down the street, then headed east. There should be a cab stand at Forty-Ninth and First and what he needed right now was a cab.

He was less than a hundred yards away from Meta's apartment when he heard a motor behind him. Turning he saw a cab coming along the street. He stepped back against the wall, saw the cab pull up, saw Stefanos get out and hurry up the steps. The gears clashed, the cab moved toward him. He ran to the edge of the sidewalk and flagged it down. He jumped inside.

'Hudson River Club,' Red told the driver. As the cab swung north on First Avenue and picked up speed Red felt fear tightening his stomach muscles. If Meta started telephoning, he was really in trouble. If he had it doped out wrong, that's what she would do instead of waiting until she talked things over with Stefanos and looked for Eels' missing body.

# CHAPTER TEN

THERE WAS little traffic on the Causeway. The cab picked up speed and the cool wind flowed in, bringing with it the smell of the river. The driver's flat voice droned on. Occasionally Red answered with a monosyllable. He thought suddenly of Ann and then he stopped worrying about what was going to happen to him. Dusk would be creeping up the shoulders of the Sierras now, softening the granite spires and bald domes. The great meadow would be a pool of darkness. So much at stake. So much to lose. The memory of the girl increased the aching anger in him. Damn them, damn them! If he lost, she would fight at first. She would be loyal at first. Then they'd move in on her – her father and mother, that lump of a game warden, the people of Bridgeport. She'd forget him after a while. And suppose he didn't lose. Suppose his plan worked. He had killed a man and if it didn't catch up to him now it might some day. The driver's voice intruded.

'Gonna do some gambling?'

'I'm toying with the idea,' Red said.

'You better be well heeled.' The driver threw a sour grin back at him.

'Tough joint?'

'Just crooked. First time for you?'

'I've been away. Who runs it?'

'Lou Baylord.'

The name meant nothing to Red. 'Who's he?'

'I wouldn't know. I don't run around in them circles. Too rich for my blood.'

'Joint wide open?'

'Night club part is. You want to gamble, you go upstairs. Baylord looks you over and if you don't smell like the law he gives you a card.'

They were crossing the bridge. Red leaned over and peered down at the river. He hoped this wouldn't be his last look at it. If Mr. Baylord was expecting him it might be.

'Always I get a kick out of this bridge,' the driver said. 'I'm queer for bridges.'

'I'm queer for rivers.' Red thought of the Kings and the West Walker and the Stanislaus and the Tuolomne. Good names to roll around your mouth. Tough, brawling streams tearing through the canyons. Why in hell did the past have to catch up with him now?

Ahead lights bloomed on the cliff. They turned off the bridge and a neon sign wrote the name of the club on the sky.

'Hold on to your watch,' said the driver. 'Here we are.'

Red handed him a ten-dollar bill. 'Stick around.'

'You can always pick up a hack here.'

'Not one driven by a guy who is queer for bridges,' Red smiled.

'Okay. I'll wait. Don't be all night.'

'Not me.' Red climbed the steps under a canopy, was bowed to by the doorman who came hurrying down, ignored the hat-check girl's request for his hat and coat, glanced into a big circular room where a tired floor show was in progress, located a stairway and went up. The feel of his gun against his leg gave him small comfort, as he found the door with Baylord's name on it. His heart was slapping against his ribs and not from climbing stairs. Here goes, he thought, and rapped on the door.

'Come in,' a man's voice told him. Nothing familiar about the voice. He opened the door, saw a middle-aged man with thinning hair and jowls standing in front of a desk. Something vaguely familiar about that face. Yet it might be because Lou Baylord looked like a thousand other men. The door clicked to behind him. He crossed the thick carpet, nodded and smiled, all the time watching the other's face, searching for some look of recognition in the hard, dark eyes.

'Mr. Baylord?'

'That's me.'

'Wynn said to look you up.'

The thin eyebrows drew together. 'Wynn?'

'Yeah. I want a card.'

'Oh,' Baylord said, still puzzled.

'You remember Wynn,' Red said, stopping in front of the man. Baylord looked up at him.

'I'm sorry –'

'So am I,' Red said and brought his fist up. Baylord's head snapped back. Red caught him with his left hand and hit him again on the jaw. Then he eased him down on the carpet, took out his gun, rapped him sharply on the temple, hurried to the door and locked it. The phone on the desk brought him back across the room. He picked it up, grunted into the mouth piece.

'Mr. Baylord,' a girl's voice said. 'Somebody just –'

'It's all right,' Red mumbled and hung up the phone.

He wasn't frightened now. Socking Baylord had driven all the fear out of him. He glanced down at the man, tried again to place him, gave it up. What he wanted was a brief case and he had better start tearing the joint apart. He went around the desk and started opening drawers.

The big bottom one wouldn't give. He yanked at it, then hunted for something to pry the lock open. A thin paper-knife broke in his hand. He tossed it away, frowned down at the desk. An idea occurred to him. He pulled out the drawer above and put it on the floor, reached through the hole and felt the lovely smoothness of leather. A moment later he was holding a brief case and on the front of the case was Lloyd Eels' name printed in gold.

Baylord groaned and tried to push himself up on his hands.

Red came around the desk and shoved his face into the carpet. Weakly Baylord tried to wriggle away. Red flipped him over, rapped him again on the temple and, when he was still, ran one hand into the man's breast pocket and brought out a fat wallet. The wallet was stuffed with bills. No use being squeamish at a time like this, Red told himself as he pocketed the wallet. He was going to need money, plenty of it, because it might be a long while before he could show himself in a bank. He shoved the gun in his coat pocket, picked up the brief case and headed for the door.

Two men in evening clothes were coming up the stairs. They stared at him coldly. Red smiled and went slowly down. He knew they had turned and were watching him but still he didn't hurry. The hat-check girl leaned on her counter. She too was watching him. He found a bill in a pants pocket, dropped it on the counter as he passed, gave her a smile and went outside. He kept his steps slow, wanting to run yet knowing that if he did all hell would break loose.

A cab motor started in the drive. His cab pulled up in front of the canopy. The doorman opened the door and stood aside. Red found another bill, shoved it in the outstretched hand and slammed the door.

'You certainly was quick,' said the driver.

'I certainly was,' said Red. 'Now see how quick you can get to Grand Central.' He threw a glance back at the door. The doorman was plodding up the steps and no one was coming down. He ran his hand lovingly over the brief case and sucked air into his lungs.

From where he stood in the arcade Red could see the information desk and most of the lower level waiting room. It was eleven o'clock and he had been waiting fifteen minutes. He tried to simulate interest in the shop window beside him but every few moments he glanced into the waiting room. His right hand was thrust into his coat pocket and his fingers were curled around the butt of his gun. When he saw the cab driver come into the waiting room carrying a suitcase

71

Red didn't move toward him right away. He waited until the driver reached the information desk, to make sure no one was following the man, then he walked briskly forward.

'All set,' the driver said. 'I hope she's all there.'

'You pack?'

'No. The bellhop. They wouldn't let me.'

'Pay the bill?'

'Sure.' He fished some money out of his pocket. 'Here's your change.'

'Keep it,' Red said and gave him another ten. 'Go out and find yourself a bridge. There are some fine covered ones in Vermount.'

The driver grinned. 'And forget I ever seen you.'

'An understanding heart,' said Red.

'Did you stick up that joint?'

'No. Should I have?'

'I sorta hoped you would,' the driver said. 'So long.'

Red watched him go away. He picked up the bag, climbed to the upper level, went through the arcade into the Biltmore lobby to the desk.

A pleasant, gray-haired man shoved a card at him. He scrawled on the card the name of a man long dead and turned to find an elderly bellhop tucking the brief case under his arm.

Red held out a hand. 'I'll take that.'

'I can manage,' the bellhop said but at Red's insistence, he grudgingly gave up the fat leather case, though he looked at it hungrily as the elevator shot them upstairs. Red, hoping the man's eyesight was bad, casually turned the case so that Eels' name was against his leg.

A cool wind pushed into the room when the bellhop opened the windows. 'Anything else, sir?' he asked.

Red gave him five dollars and told him to rustle up some wrapping paper and string. The man's gnarled fingers caressed the bill. He smiled respectfully and went out.

Excitement made Red's hands clumsy as he worked on the lock with a fingernail file. Presently the lock gave and he

72

pulled out the thick pile of stapled onion-skin paper, stared down at the neat typescript and the row on row of figures, flipped the thin pages and saw names and dates. When the bellhop rapped softly on the door Red knew why Lloyd Eels was dead.

The bellhop put a folded sheet of brown manila paper and some heavy string in Red's outstretched hand. 'Thank you,' Red said and closed and locked the door.

He went back to the bed and stood looking down at the sheaf of documents that had cost a man his life. He wondered at his blindness.

Now he remembered where he had seen Lou Baylord before. Now he remembered snow drifting past a window and a man with a bullet hole in his belly and a thin, soft-voiced man with a copy of *North of Boston* in his hand. Lou, Whit Sterling had called him.

There was no anger in Red any more. He had double-crossed Sterling and Lloyd Eels must have double-crossed him too. Apparently you couldn't do it and get away with it. He felt a vast surprise at Sterling's capacity for revenge.

On the bed lay Sterling's one-way ticket to Alcatraz. Sterling wanted it and Red didn't blame him. Eels had done a job of digging – too good a job. He had dug himself right into Woodlawn Cemetery. And me with him unless I move fast, Red told himself.

He had a handful of dynamite to heave at Sterling. He had evidence that the gambler had evaded some three million dollars in income tax. But there was one thing he didn't have – one thing he must have if he wanted to keep on living – the affidavit accusing him of murder and bearing Mumsie's name tucked away in the safe in Lloyd Eel's office.

# CHAPTER ELEVEN

THROUGH THE window Petey Berg could see the bridge spanning the river – the long cables like webs of silver in the moonlight. But he didn't care about bridges now. All he wanted to do was to get the hell away from this place. Jesus, why hadn't he gone home? Why had he waited around hoping to pick up a few extra bucks before midnight?

Blood oozed across one cheek. He took out a dirty handkerchief and dabbed at it and stabbing pain cleared some of the fog from his mind.

'You ready to talk?' Lou Baylord asked. Baylord's bruised, swollen face moved into the cab driver's line of vision. Behind Baylord stood the two men who had walked up to the hack stand around the corner from the Gotham Hotel, climbed into the cab then shoved guns in his back and told him to take them to the Hudson River Club. One was a little Greek with thick, soft lips. The other was a string bean of a man who looked like an undertaker.

What the hell! the cab driver told himself. Why get your brains beat out for a guy you never saw before – a guy who didn't give a damn what happened to a hack driver named Petey Berg?

'Yeah, I picked him up,' Petey admitted.

'Why didn't you say so before?' Baylord hit him with the back of his hand.

'Don't,' Petey protested dully. 'Don't do that any more. He told me not to. He gave me a saw back to clam up.'

74

Baylord made a threatening gesture. 'No, Lou,' the thin guy said. 'He's just a poor dumb son of a bitch.'

'I'm running this.' Baylord turned angry eyes on the thin guy.

'Wait and take it out on that red bastard,' the thin guy advised.

'I'll talk,' Petey said. 'Ain't no sense in me not.'

'Where'd you take him?' Baylord asked.

'Grand Central. Then I went back to the St. Regis and paid his bill and got his bag. Took it to the waiting room. I didn't see him no more after that.'

'He take a train?'

'I don't know. Ain't no trains I know of but locals that time of night. Maybe he took a local. Maybe he got himself another hotel room. Commodore and Biltmore are handy.'

'You sure used up a lot of our time,' Baylord said.

'Principles, that's why,' Petey answered. 'You give me dough to clam up, I clam up.'

The thin guy fumbled in his pocket, found a bill, tossed it in Petey's lap. 'For your principles, Buster.'

'No.' Baylord reached for the bill. 'There's better ways.'

'Use your head.' The thin guy took Baylord's arm and led him over to a corner. Petey heard them mumbling but he couldn't make any sense out of the mumbling. The little Greek came over, put a cigarette between his lips and lighted it. 'Thanks,' Petey said. The thin guy came back, put one hand on Petey's shoulder and grinned down at him.

'Mr. Baylord is all for dumping you off the bridge,' the thin guy said. He's a little out of sorts tonight.'

'Shut up!' Baylord snapped.

'Like I said he is out of sorts,' the thin guy said. 'Your red-headed fare worked him over.'

'You and your goddamned cracks.' Baylord started for him, changed his mind and directed his anger at Petey.

'Maybe tomorrow or next day the cops will pick you up. Okay. You clam up about us. Get it?'

'I get it.'

'Just forget certain things,' the thin guy suggested. 'Like bringing the redhead out here. You picked him up. He had a tan brief case with him and you seen a name on the case. Lloyd Eel's name. Go on from there. The St. Regis. Grand Central. And that's all.' His voice got thin and sharp. He looked more than ever like an undertaker.

'You want to know why?' Baylord asked.

'I don't want to know anything,' Petey said.

'Let's go,' the thin guy said. 'Drop us off at Grand Central on your way home.'

Petey got weakly to his feet. Through the window he looked at the river and at the bridge spanning the river. Now the bridge was a thing to be afraid of, ugly and threatening. He closed his eyes to clear the dizziness from his brain.


Red's footsteps echoed through the empty ill-lighted street. As he approached the alleyway leading past the church, he moved more softly. Walking on the balls of his feet he went down the alleyway to the fence and cautiously pulled himself up. The lights were on in Meta's apartment and he could see through the glass doors into the big room. There was no one in the room.

He swung over into the courtyard and tiptoed forward across the wet bricks. His gun was ready in one hand. Meta might be in the bedroom and Joe Stefanos might be waiting with her. Or they might be in the building on Central Park South trying to find Eels' body. The door was locked. His passkey opened it and he stepped quietly inside.

No one in the bedroom. No one anywhere. He considered sitting down, having a drink and waiting for her then put the idea aside. He had wasted too much time already, could afford to waste no more. That hour he had spent in Eels' office trying to crack a safe with nothing but his bare hands had netted him nothing of value. Unless you could call finding out that Eels had once been Whit Sterling's attorney valuable. That was interesting. That helped you look on Eels' murder more realistically. But it didn't get you out of the spot you were in.

He found the telephone directory in a drawer of the desk, got the number of the Hudson River Club and dialed.

'Lou Baylord, please,' he said when a girl's low voice answered.

'Who's calling?'

'It's about a brief case. Tell him that. He'll understand.'

He sat on the corner of the desk, holding his gun in one hand and the receiver in the other, watching the door that led into the hall. He hoped Stefanos wouldn't show up for a while because then he would have to shoot the little Greek and all the cops in town would come barging into the joint.

The telephone came to life. Baylord's voice asked, 'Who is this?'

'Red Bailey.'

'You bastard,' Baylord said.

'Don't you want the Eels' file back?'

Baylord didn't answer for a minute. Red wondered if Stefanos had reported to him yet. But he didn't ask. It really didn't matter.

'Well, don't you?' Red insisted.

'Yes.' Baylord replied grudgingly. 'How do I get it?'

'Put Meta Carson on the phone.'

'She isn't here.'

'Then scare her up,' Red said. 'Tell her to go to Eels' office and get that affidavit out of the safe. Tell her to bring it to the information desk in the lower level waiting room at Grand Central. Alone. I'll be around somewhere watching. I'll have the brief case. We make a trade.'

Baylord cursed him softly but very fluently.

Red decided to surprise him. 'I'll even tell you where Eels' body is. You might want to keep it away from the cops.'

There was no exclamation of surprise at the other end of the wire. So Baylord knew. He had been in touch with Stefanos and Meta.

'I don't trust you,' Baylord said at last.

'I want the affidavit. I don't give a damn about the brief case.'

'Tell you what I'll do,' Baylord replied. I'll meet you in Grand Central.'

'No.'

Baylord's tone changed. 'Now look here, Red. I got to have that file. You know what a spot I'm in. And from here out I ain't trusting nobody. How do I know you won't run out with the brief case as soon as you get your hand on the affidavit? I want to be there.'

'You'll be alone?'

'Sure.'

It sounded reasonable enough. Red didn't blame Baylord for being suspicious, for not trusting him. Certainly he had never done anything to prove himself worthy of Baylord's trust.

'All right. But keep your hands out of your pockets. Come in from the Lexington Avenue side and don't have any boys tagging along.'

'I won't.'

'Get going.' Red said. 'I want to leave town.' He hung up, wiped the sweat from his forehead and got off the desk. The whisky bottle was still on the coffee table. He poured out a generous drink, downed it and went out into the courtyard.

It was dark there, dark and cool. For a while he considered waiting. Too tough a place to get out of if things went wrong. Someone could come up the alleyway from Forty-Seventh Street and he'd be sunk. So he crossed to the wall, dropped lightly over and hurried away, this time caring not at all if anyone heard him.

Ten minutes later he lounged in an entryway across from the Graybar Building, watching the entrance through which presently Meta Carson would hurry – unless his luck ran out. It wouldn't. He was confident of that now. By morning he would be on a plane and the plane would be heading west. Tomorrow he would hold Ann in his arms again. He grinned up through the dark canyon at the pale strip of sky.

Not half a mile away another man stood in a dark entryway, scanning the names under the mailboxes. Finding the one he sought he put a finger on the bell and waited for the answering buzz that would admit him.

# CHAPTER TWELVE

AUGUST TILLOTSON threw off the blanket of sleep, sat up and padded groggily across the littered room to the door. His finger found the button that would release the catch downstairs. He pushed it, grumbling sleepily, hitching up his rumpled pajamas and pulling the drawstring tighter around his flabby middle.

Knuckles rapped on the door. Tillotson flicked on the light, opened the door a crack and peered out. A policeman stood in the hall. A deep respect for law and order made Tillotson suddenly humble. He forgot his annoyance at being awakened at his ungodly hour and said, 'How do you do?'

'One of your tenants is upset,' the policeman explained. 'He says some dame was screaming on the fourth floor.'

'There are no ladies on the fourth floor,' said Tillotson. 'Only Mr. Eels.'

'This guy called about an hour ago,' the policeman said. 'They just got around to telling me. Maybe they ain't nothing to it but suppose we take a look just for ducks.'

'I hate to disturb him.' Then Mr. Tillotson remembered the telephone call from Miss Carson earlier in the evening so he donned a worn flannel bathrobe and slippers, got his keys and escorted the policeman upstairs.

Apologetically he thumbed the bell. There was no answer so he pushed it again and again. Then timidly he put the passkey in the lock and opened the door.

The room was dark, save for what little light was cast through the open windows by the waning moon.

'Mr. Eels,' Tillotson called softly. 'Oh, Mr. Eels. It's me.' The policeman pushed past him, barged forward then stumbled and said 'Jesus Keerist.' Tillotson flipped on the lights.

'Oh, dear!' said Tillotson. Meta Carson was sprawled on the carpet. He didn't have to look twice to know she was dead. He turned away sick and shaken and would have run into the hall had not the policeman stopped him.

'Stick around,' the policeman ordered. He dropped on one knee beside the girl's body. 'Blunt instrument,' he said sagely, gingerly touching her cold cheek. 'Dead maybe an hour. Now you was speaking of a Mr. Eels. This obviously ain't him.'

'His secretary,' Tillotson said weakly. 'Her name is Meta Carson. She called me tonight.' He paused, remembering the call, telling himself it was all very strange.

'Oh, she did?'

Tillotson nodded. He repeated his thoughts aloud. The policeman took out a book and made notes, mumbling as he wrote. Meanwhile Tillotson was looking around the disordered room. A chair lay overturned. Papers were strewn around and where the picture had been pushed aside the wall safe gaped open. He pointed. The policeman indicated that he was quite aware of things. He wrote a number down, tore out the page and handed it to Tillotson.

'Run on downstairs and call that number. Say there's been a murder. I don't want to use the phone up here.'

It took all his will power to get him across the shadowy, badly lighted hall to the waiting elevator. He glanced back at the policeman standing in the doorway, summoned up his courage and closed the door. The policeman turned and began a methodical search of the apartment. Now he had his gun in one hand and he, too, knew what fear was. He found the balcony door, opened it and went out and along it to the iron fence that separated Eels' balcony from the one leading into the next apartment. He stepped over the fence, flashed his light through curtainless windows into the vacant apartment, tried the door. It gave under his hand. He stepped inside and played his light around. Finding nothing but evidence of work in progress he returned to Eels' messy abode.

Tillotson, his hands stuck in the pockets of his robe to stop their trembling, returned and watched the policeman as he continued his search. A portable typewriter stood on the desk by the telephone and when the policeman, now killing time until the boys from homicide showed up, opened it he saw the paper and read the typed script.

'If anything happens to me there's a document in the safe in my office that is self-explanatory.' Eels' name was typed under the brief note.

'It don't say nothing about if anything happened to the dame, however,' the policeman observed, cocking his head at Tillotson. 'And that is who something happened to. It looks like the homicide boys'll be very busy for a while.'


A police car slammed to a stop in front of the Graybar Building, then another. Men got out and hurried inside. Red, standing in the shadows, watched them and figured his luck had run out. A feeling of hopelessness and helplessness held him there in the entryway. He had been too sure of himself, too certain of his own omnipotence. A moment later a cab pulled up behind the police cars and four men, one carrying a camera case, spilled out and started for the door only to be stopped by a policeman.

Angry voices drifted across to Red. The men wanted to go in and no cop was going to stop them.

'Simmer down,' the policeman said. 'Ain't the dame being dead enough for you guys?'

Dame? So that was it. Then there was still a chance. Red started out of the shadows but stopped as another cab came from the other direction. It started to turn and he heard a voice say, 'No, go on.' Two men occupied the back seat.

One of them was Baylord. The cab drew away and vanished around the corner.

Then the presence of the law was none of Baylord's planning. Baylord had been headed for Eels' office and those waiting police cars had scared him off. Now what? Well, he still had his bundle of dynamite and there must be some way to use it. And he still had time – not much but enough to put many miles between himself and New York. His agile mind put things together. The dame must be Meta and maybe they were looking for Eels. If they were, until they found his body Red was safe. Safe, that is, from the law. But not from Whit Sterling. Not from Baylord. Until Sterling got his hands on that file, Red would never be safe. Even then his life was a bad insurance risk.

Keeping in the shadow of the buildings he sauntered slowly to the corner. It seemed to him his footsteps filled the whole street with sound. Around the corner he moved faster and often he glanced back. But no one followed him and presently he found a cab. The driver dozed over the wheel. Red had to shake him to wake him up.

'Biltmore,' Red said.

'Whyn't you walk?' the driver grumbled.

'From there we go places.'

Grudgingly the driver motioned to the door. When Red got in he slammed the cab gear as though taking out on the aged mechanism his anger against his fare.

The night clerk dozed behind the desk. Red's glance embraced the lobby. No one waiting for him but he mustn't take chances. He crossed to the bank of house phones, gave the girl the number of his room, waited a little. When there was no answer he took an up elevator. Caution made him wary. He unlocked the door, kicked it open then stood aside with his right hand gripping the gun in the pocket of his raincoat. He reached in and flipped on the lights. Empty. His bag stood open on the stand as he had left it. Quickly he closed and locked the door, took a quick look in the closet and bathroom, then picked up the phone and told the night clerk to get his bill ready and send a bellboy up.

There was nothing much to pack – his razor, toothbrush, a few toilet articles. Before he closed the bag he tried to remember how things had been arranged, but could not. If someone had searched his room it had been done carefully. Yet he mustn't take chances, mustn't make the mistake of underestimating Whit Sterling. From now on there would be someone forever at his heels. Momentarily he considered sitting down and waiting for them. Get it over with. Call up the cops and say, 'I'm the guy you'll be looking for presently.' Call Baylord, stir things up and take a chance that you'd come out of the mess with a second-degree murder rap.

He thought of Ann and put the idea aside. Too much to lose. Knuckles beat a sharp tattoo on the door. Still cautious, he opened it. A sleepy bellhop pushed past him, picked up his bag and, unsmilingly as though annoyed at life, led the way to the elevators.

'You didn't stay long,' the night clerk said as he took Red's money and stamped the bill. 'Leaving town?'

Red nodded. 'Under the desk there's a brief case.'

The night clerk found it, put it on the desk. Now it no longer bore Lloyd Eels' name. A knife blade had scarred the leather deeply. Red thanked him, tucked it under one arm and followed the bellhop out to the waiting cab.

A quiet emptiness filled the street yet a threatening undercurrent seemed flowing through the silence.

'Now where?' the driver asked, as Red got in.

Red's voice was low. 'La Guardia Field.'

The bellhop chose that moment to stick his head inside the cab and thank Red for his tip. Maybe he heard the order, maybe he didn't. Anyway it couldn't be helped.

The cab rattled through the empty canyons, the driver bending over the wheel as though the trip required tremendous concentration – not speaking, apparently still hating wakefulness. The tunnel swallowed them. Red thought of the dirty river swirling above them and the depression that settled on him was not lifted when he felt clean wind and saw the city again. Occasionally he glanced back. Sometimes headlights showed behind then fell away. Safe for a little while but not for long. They would pick up his trail and follow him. All he could do until he was ready to move in on Sterling was cover up his tracks as best he could. Well, he knew a place they wouldn't think of looking and that's where he was headed.

Few people were in the waiting room. He sought a familiar face but found none, crossed to the ticket window and asked an overly genial clerk about planes. No flights for the coast until morning. But there was a plane for Cleveland in ten minutes. That, Red said, would do. He handed over his grip and brief case, casting nervous glances toward the entrance. Pocketing his ticket he went outside and found a bit of darkness near the gate. Three cheerful drunks were telling a fourth how sorry they were to have him leave. A man and woman stood close together whispering gravely. Out on the field lights bloomed around a moth-like silver plane and monkey-figures clambered over it.

Two men came along the walk and took their places near the gate. Momentarily Red pressed back against the fence until they turned their faces toward him and he knew they were strangers. Then the gate opened and he joined the small hurrying procession to the waiting plane.

His seat was forward and through the window he could see the gate. Relaxed now he sat there watching. A smaller gate stood beyond. Through it came a uniformed attendant pushing a cart loaded with baggage. The man stopped just inside the gate to pitch a cigarette away. Light from the battery of flood-lamps fell on the cart. Red could see his bag and the brief case resting on it. Now instead of watching the gate he was watching the cart.

The attendant started forward. Something moved behind him. A man sprang at him, pushed him aside, snatched the brief case from the cart and raced away through the gate and along the fence to disappear. The attendant emitted a yell and leaped in pursuit. There was bedlam on the field.

Ten minutes later, when the baggage was aboard and the door was closed and the big ship was taxiing down the field, the stewardess moved down the aisle to stand beside Red.

'I'm sorry,' the stewardess said. 'I think someone stole your brief case.'

Red grinned at her. 'He's welcome to it. It may bring him salvation.'

The girl eyed him with frowning curiosity.

'There were two Gideon Bibles in it,' Red said.

Lou Baylord pulled back to hurl the Bibles at Joe Stefanos, but the thin guy standing behind Lou grabbed his arm.

'Don't go heaving them books around,' the thin guy said. 'I'm superstitious.' He took the Bibles, put them gently on the window sill and stood looking south and east across the river. Dawn wasn't far away and the buildings were like cardboard cutouts against the pale sky.

Deprived of his missile Lou hurled a name at Joe. 'You Greek son of a bitch!'

Joe got slowly off his chair, shoved his hands deep in his pockets and started across the room. 'Don't call me that.'

The thin guy turned and stood grinning at them both. 'He's sensitive about being a Greek.'

'Shut up!' Joe said. 'Who let him walk out with it in the first place?'

'Lou,' replied the thin guy. 'Cool off, Joseph. You've been doing fine. Outside of losing a stiff and stealing from the Gideons you've been doing perfect. Now let go of that cannon because we can't go around knocking each other off. Whit wouldn't like it.'

Joe had a vulgar suggestion as to what Whit and Lou and the thin guy could do. But he took his hands out of his pockets and went back to his chair. 'I don't have to take any crap off you dopes. Guy Parker's my boss.'

'And he'll give you a gold star,' said the thin guy.

86

'How can I think with you birds gabbing all the time?' Lou growled. 'What do the morning papers say?'

'Not much,' the thin guy replied. 'Because this is Sunday and murders don't get much play on the Sabbath. They are looking for Eels. They don't say he killed her but they hint at it. Then they turn around and say maybe he met with foul play too.'

'He sure did,' said Joe. 'I wonder what that bastard did with him.'

'Put him in the icebox maybe.'

'I looked.'

'What else?' Lou disregarded Joe.

'If Eels don't show up they are going to open his safe,' the thin guy said. 'Until they do, two guys armed with machine guns, hand grenades, tear gas and I don't know what the hell else are parked in Eels' office.'

'Papers say that?' Lou scowled across at the thin guy. He hoped it wasn't true. He wanted very much to get that affidavit because right now Red had the dice and was throwing sevens. Lou didn't like to make deals but there were times when you had to. This looked like one of them. The thin guy nodded. Lou puffed out his cheeks. 'Maybe when they go out to lunch you could sneak in there and blow the safe.'

'Not me. You couldn't get past the front door. If you did there's the elevator. Guy running it keeps track of everybody going up and down. That's how they know she was in there last night. And about the brief case. The cops are very familiar with our pusses and we don't want to get our names in the paper – do we?'

'No.' Lou turned his smoldering, angry gaze on Joe but he spoke gently. 'I wish to hell you had waited to kill her.'

Joe shrugged. 'So I didn't.'

'So we're screwed,' said Lou mildly, reaching for the phone. He told the girl to put in a call for Guy Parker, put the instrument back on its cradle and began cleaning his nails with the broken blade of the paper knife. The thin guy yawned, glanced at the sky.

'Sun will be up pretty soon,' the thin guy said. 'Maybe we ought to go out to Jones Beach for a swim.'

'Maybe we ought,' agreed Lou. 'But we aren't going to. There are a few minor items to attend to.' Through narrowed lids he smiled at Joe. 'Like finding Eels' body and getting Red before he decides to be patriotic.'

He rose, stood beside the thin guy and stared moodily down at the river. His silence was more menacing than his speech had been. The sun was thinking about coming up, tinting the sky while it dawdled beyond the rim of sea.

The phone bell recalled Lou. Across a continent a tall, gray man sat at his desk, the receiver cradled against his shoulder so he could play with a deck of cards. He listened without comment, as Lou Baylord told him what was up. The gray man's pleasant expression didn't change throughout the one-sided conversation. When Lou was done, Guy Parker said, 'Tell Joe to come on home. I'm going to need him.'

'You can have him,' Lou said. He put the phone down, yawned and stretched. The two men watched him with hard, blank faces.

The sun looked in on them for a moment then slid away.

'You better go too, Slats,' said Lou. 'Joe needs a nursemaid.'

'The name is Christopher,' the thin guy said.

# CHAPTER THIRTEEN

THE HULKING Negro doorman watched the Model A Ford roadster rattling along the graveled drive. When it stopped he made no move to open the door. The sole occupant was a wizened youth in jeans and a blue shirt who sat behind the wheel staring up at the white facade of the El Arbol Rancho as though trying to make up his mind about something. Daylight still clung to the hills and, save for the doorman, the place seemed deserted.

Slowly the doorman moved down the steps but his ugly scowl had no effect on the driver of the battered car. 'What you want?' the doorman asked.

The Kid turned his attention from the pillared porch and gave it slowly and blankly to the doorman.

'Get that junk heap out of here,' the doorman ordered.

Understanding came into the Kid's pale blue eyes as he watched the doorman's thick lips move. He took a folded paper from his shirt pocket and handed it to the Negro, who squinted down at it, then lost his threatening look. He slid in beside the Kid and pointed up ahead to the empty parking lot under the poplar trees. The smile he gave the Kid was gently sympathetic.

The Kid smiled back, put the car in gear and drove on around the bend. He parked it against a tree. Both men got out. The Negro led the way around to the back, through a door into a long dark hallway and along the hall to a narrow stairway. He motioned to the Kid to wait at the foot of the stairs, went up and along another hall to a door and rapped gently. Guy Parker's voice told him to come in and he obeyed. Now humble as he closed the door behind him he went slowly across the big, comfortably furnished sitting room to the windowed alcove where Parker was eating what was to him breakfast.

'Mister Parker, sir, they's a dummy wants to see you,' the doorman said.

'A what?' Parker was reading a magazine as he ate and he didn't look up.

'A dummy.'

Parker filled his mouth with ham, then slowly gave his frowning attention to the doorman. He said, 'Make sense, you black bastard.'

'A deef and dumb boy,' the doorman said. 'A dummy.'

'How do you know he wants to see me if he can't talk?'

The doorman held out the piece of paper on which were scrawled nine words. Still annoyed at being interrupted, Parker took it. Suddenly he jumped up, almost upsetting the table.

'Send him up,' Parker snapped. 'Then wake Joe and tell him to get the hell in here.'

'Yassuh, boss,' the Negro said, nodding and smiling as he backed toward the door. Outside he dropped the cloak of humility, threw a crooked, sneering smile at the closed door and went down to where the kid waited. He put a gentle hand on the Kid's shoulder and motioned to the stairway.

'First door you come to,' he said. Then remembering the Kid's affliction he shepherded him up, mumbling to himself. He rapped again, opened the door for the Kid and, inside, pulled the door shut. He went in search of Joe Stefanos.

Parker was across the room almost before the door closed. He grabbed the Kid's shirt front and scowled down at the thin, scarred face. His cool, deadly eyes hunted for some expression of fear in the pale blue eyes of the youth. Roughly he shook the Kid, as though with force to pass a miracle and make him vocal.

90

'Where is he?' Parker said.

The pale eyes followed the movement of his lips. The Kid's thin, strong hand brushed Parker's fingers off. From his hip pocket he took an envelope and gave it to the gambler.

Parker ripped it open. Inside there were two sheets of cheap, ruled note paper covered with penciled words. When he read the first few lines he glanced at the Kid and his expression was one of angry helplessness. For Red had written:

Dear Guy:

There's no use putting lighted matches under his toenails or kicking him in the groin or trying any of your gentle tricks on him. All the art of persuasion you picked up as a copper is useless. Because he never learned to write.

'That dirty red bastard!' Parker said. He went to the leather armchair where a floor lamp burned, dropped into it and continued reading. The Kid stood watching and though his expression was blank his eyes danced with suppressed laughter.

This is Tuesday. Certainly by now Baylord will have been in touch with you. Things, you much admit, have not gone according to schedule. I have no delusions about the spot I'm in – or will be in when Eels' body is found. It will be shortly. The frame-up was a good one and I'm sorry that your satisfaction in it had to be spoiled. I do not intend, however, to stay in a spot.

There is one man who can get me out – Whit Sterling. I want to see him and I am leaving it up to you to make the arrangements. If he's in New York get him out here. You've made it impossible for me to go to him there. Call him. Find out when I can see him and send word to me through the Kid.

I have made arrangements to have Eels' information

about Sterling turned over to the Feds, if your boys start pushing me or any friend of mine around. Hurry this up.

Parker reread the letter. Rising, he moved toward the Kid, his fists clenched, his face taut with an anger that must be vented on someone. He pulled his fist back, lashed out at the Kid, who moved his head slightly and let the blow go by.

'Goddamn you!' Parker yelled and wrapped a long arm around the Kid's neck. The Kid slid out of his grasp, ran over and picked up Red's letter. His forefinger pointed to the last few lines and he stood there tapping the page with his finger and shaking his head. Parker understood. Parker said, 'So you can read, you little son of a bitch.' The Kid read his lips and nodded.

'And you can hear too, you shamming bastard.'

The Kid indicated his lips. The Kid shook his head vigorously and pointed to Parker's mouth.

'Oh,' Parker said. He formed words distinctly. 'Where's Red?'

The Kid shrugged.

Behind Parker the door opened. Joe Stefanos came in, rubbing sleep from his eyes. Joe saw the Kid and recognized him.

'Red's dummy,' Joe said, grinning. 'You'll play hell makin' him talk.' As he started past Parker the gambler slammed his fist against the side of Joe's head and sent him sprawling. Joe lay on the thick carpet shaking his head and turned cold eyes on Parker. He said softly, 'You shouldn't do that, Guy.'

Parker stood over him and drew back one foot to kick him. The expression on Joe's face made him think better of it. 'Get up.'

Joe scrambled to his feet, rubbing soft fingers across his temple and wetting his lips.

'Sorry.' Parker's anger was driven out of him by the murderous look in Joe's eyes. 'I had to hit someone.'

92

'Sure,' Joe said, giving his attention to the Kid.

'Leave him alone,' said Parker. He got the letter from the Kid and handed it to Joe, who read it without comment.

'Ain't that something!' Parker made his voice pleasant. 'He thinks he's going to get away with it.'

Joe folded the letter neatly and smiled cruelly at Parker. 'Maybe he is.'

Parker considered that. He saw the Kid watching him and sensing the amusement behind the thin, scarred mask of a face, he made a threatening gesture. But the Kid refused to show fear.

'Called Whit yet?' Joe asked.

Parker shook his head.

'Better get it over with.' Joe evidenced satisfaction from the thought of how Sterling was going to take it.

'Who's handling this?'

'You are, thank Christ,' said Joe.

Parker turned his back to the Kid. 'He can read lips, so watch out. I'm giving him a letter to take to Red. You tail him. We get our hands on the bastard and he won't be so cocky. He isn't far away, that's certain.

'Me, I'd call Whit.' Joe put a cigarette in his long holder, and lighted it. 'He wants that junk bad. Maybe had enough to make a deal.'

'You know what deal Red will make?'

Joe's shrug indicated he didn't care.

'A patsy to hang some murders on.'

The Greek put one hand in his pocket. 'It won't be me.'

'Don't be too sure.'

'I said it won't be me.' His voice was flat, deadly in its monotony.

'Then get the lead out of your can,' Parker said. 'And don't mess this up like you did the other.' He went to the small, carved desk against the wall under a Picasso print, found paper and pen and started writing. The Kid watched him and Joe watched the Kid. Darkness outside moved in swiftly and the crop of stars ripened. Night cooled the wind

93

a little. Faintly the sound of the waking establishment drifted up through the open windows.

Parker thrust an envelope in the Kid's hand and watched him tuck it in the hip pocket of his faded jeans. 'Take that to him,' he said.

The Kid nodded. The Kid looked over at Joe, pointed with his thumb and shook his head, then studied Parker's face again.

'We won't try to follow you,' Parker said.

The Kid smiled. His pale blue eyes were gleeful and Parker knew what the expression in them meant. Joe would play hell following the Kid to where Red Bailey was hiding. He motioned to the door, the Kid smiled at them both and went out and down the stairs.

Joe reached the door before Parker spoke.

'No use. He's wise,' Parker said. 'I got a better idea.'

In the back country a thunderstorm grumbled around the bald domes and across the barren, rocky wastes. But in the little meadow near where the Sonora Pass road forked from the main highway to follow the West Walker toward its source, moonlight spilled down. A dirty tent was pitched in the meadow near the river and a small fire burned in front of the tent. Red Bailey lay beside the fire, his head pillowed on his hands, looking at the sky and listening to the ominous voice of the far storm. For once in his life he found no peace in the sound of thunder in the hills. Another storm was brewing for him – he knew that. But what he didn't know was that the storm had already broken.

Lloyd Eels' body lay in the morgue in New York City and the medical examiner methodically worked over it. In an offics not far away men read Mumsie McGonigle's affidavit and men put bits and pieces of evidence together.

Before morning the hunt for Red Bailey would be on. Papers would tell the world about him. Wires would carry the story swiftly west and presently a car would scream up the American River to turn off at Strawberry. Men would get out of it and go up to another meadow and start hunting for the long-hidden grave of Jack Fisher.

The fire was dead but still Red did not sleep. The night had a bite to it. He pulled the canvas over him and lay listening for the sound of a car on the far road, hearing instead the chuckle of the river through the rocks and a lonely coyote on the mountain.

Another hour passed and now there was no moonlight. Red got up and went across the meadow to where a rutted dirt road found its way through the forest and along the road to the highway. He climbed the bank, hunched down behind a stunted pine and waited. He felt a thrust of fear. Perhaps he had been wrong dragging the Kid into this. A selfish thing to do. A cruel thing to do really. Like selling gold bricks in a school for the blind.

Yet the Kid had wanted to help, had insisted on helping. When Red slipped into the house back of the service station last night, the Kid had known, without being told, that Red was in a jam. Those nimble fingers of his had questioned him until Red told the story, glad of someone he could trust to tell it to. The Kid's fingers had made letters and the letters had made words and the gist of it had been that the Kid would be the contact between Red and Parker.

'They may beat the hell out of you,' Red had said. A shrug had been the Kid's reply.

A dummy, people called him. Red wished that all men including himself were as intelligent. The ears might not hear and the lips might not speak but eternal silence seemed to give the Kid a second sight.

Lights rounded a bend to the north, came closer. Red looked into the cut and saw a small car. He scrambled down the bank and was waiting where the dirt road joined the highway when the car stopped and the Kid got out. The Kid didn't start for the meadow at once. He stood by the roadside making sure no one was following him. Presently he got back in the car, turned into the dirt road and parked it behind some brush.

In the tent Red lighted the gasoline lantern and read Parker's short message. Sterling was in California and Parker would talk to him. It was up to Sterling whether or not Red could see him. He'd send a message down to the service station when Sterling made up his mind.

Red looked up from the letter. 'They push you around?'

The Kid's fingers told him what had happened. As the fingers talked the Kid's eyes danced.

Red put one hand on the Kid's shoulder and squeezed it. 'Thanks, Kid.'

The Kid looked up at him and his fingers asked a question: Was Red sure he didn't want Ann to know that he was here?

'The less she knows the safer she is,' Red replied. 'Not a word now.'

The Kid nodded agreement and again his fingers spoke. He'd keep an eye on her. He'd see nothing happened to her.

Red thanked him, put the lantern out and walked with him to the car. He hated to see the Kid drive away because now he was lonely and that was something he had never been before.

# Chapter Fourteen

Ann Miller's bedroom faced west and the first thing she saw when she slid out of bed was the wall of the hills. They made her think of Red, which wasn't odd. Everything – the fields, the creeks, the wind, the stars – brought the thought of him welling up until the longing for him was unbearable. She stood at the window, shivering a little because the sun wasn't high enough yet to warm the wind. The cotton gown her mother had made for her covered her slim body primly and made her look even younger than she was. She looked down at the gown and wondered why she wore the thing. Just because her mother insisted was no reason.

It was time she took her life out of her mother's hands. Mother was sweet and father was sweet but why should they keep on insisting that she was a child and had to be told what to do and what to wear? Briefly she allowed herself to be annoyed at them. Then she pushed the feeling aside. Unworthy. There were fine and kind and thoughtful. They just didn't understand, that was all. And how could they? They couldn't see him as she saw him because they didn't know him. They would though. And when they did they'd love him too.

The fields were bright with sun. Over by the ditch some quail were being very angry about something. Probably a cat. Oh, she felt good today, too good to sit at her desk and type dull letters and listen to her father settling the problems of the world with anyone who stuck his head in the door. This was a day for a picnic – walking along a creek with him, lying on the warm sand close to him, hearing his deep voice and his laughter. *Oh, Red*, she thought, *hurry back, hurry back!*

A small fear nudged her heart. He hadn't written. Only a wire the day he reached New York. But then he must be busy. He must be hurrying to get things done so he could come back to her.

Her mother's voice drifted up from the kitchen. 'Ann. Are you up?'

She leaned out. 'Yes, mother.'

'Hurry, dear.'

'Yes, mother.'

The back door slammed. Her father crossed the yard, looked up and waved. She blew a kiss at him, turned and pulled the thin garment over her head.

In the mirror she could see only part of her body and that part didn't please her. Too thin. Much too thin. A child's body, the breasts no bigger than teacups. But Red loved her. And – though the knowledge didn't make her warm inside, it pleased her – Jimmy Caldwell loved her and wanted her. So there was a place in the world for the undeveloped. She grinned at herself, thinking how shocked her mother would be at all this. She ran into the bathroom and jumped under the shower.

Quickly she dressed, humming softly the while. Panties, no brassiere – some day she hoped she'd need one – a slip, sweater and skirt. No stockings. At least, she thought as she applied the brush, her hair had a nice sheen to it and it curled by itself. And her skin was good. Too many freckles perhaps but they went away in the winter.

'Ann!' her mother insisted.

'Coming.' She ran downstairs and out to the kitchen, threw her arms around her mother and kissed her. 'Good morning.' She took her place on the bench in the breakfast nook and slid her napkin out of its silver ring. At that moment her father came in with the morning paper. His face was set and his eyes had anger in them.

98

'Look at this!' Canby Miller said and he was shouting. 'My God, will you look at this!'

'Canby,' Mrs. Miller's tone reproved him.

Almost triumphantly he spread the paper on the table and stood there shaking a finger at the headline. Ann read it and closed her eyes. She wouldn't look. If she kept her eyes shut for a while everything would be all right. Those words would change into other words and everything would be all right. Her mother moaned. 'Ann, Ann! Oh, my God! Oh, my God!' There was no sympathy for the girl in her tone. There was only horror that such a thing could have happened to them.

'I knew it,' Canby said. 'I knew he was no good. I said all along there's a man who should be run out of town.'

Suddenly he stopped talking and stared down at his daughter. Pity fought its way up, fought past the knowledge that it would be a long time before he could walk through Bridgeport with his head held high. The poor kid, he thought, the poor *little kid*.

He put out a hand and touched her shoulder. Ann opened her eyes. There on the table was the paper screaming at her:

### RED BAILEY HUNTED FOR MURDER
Bridgeport Service Station Operator Sought in Double New York Slaying; Attorney and Secretary His Victims; Old Crime Motive, Police Say.

Ann rose, pushed past her father and walked blindly through the back door and out across the yard.

Jim Caldwell saw them looking at him when he came into the cafe – the three men hunched over the counter, the plump, vacant-faced waitress, Pop Wise who owned the joint. Each face had the same excited, expectant expression. It was Pop who spoke first.

'Hear about Red Bailey?' Pop asked.

'What about him?' Caldwell said, trying to be casual. He

put his Stetson on one of the hooks by the door, found an empty place at the counter, reached for a menu.

'Better oil up that gun of yours,' Pop said. 'He'll be coming this way.'

'Suppose he does,' Caldwell said. 'What's it to me?'

The waitress giggled. She was so excited she couldn't stand still. 'He killed three people,' she shrilled.

Caldwell dropped the menu, stared around him.

'Listen to this,' Pop said, putting on a pair of steel-rimmed spectacles. He had the paper spread out in front of him and he bent down and started reading aloud in a strangely artificial voice.

'Red Bailey, Bridgeport service station operator, today was the object of a nation-wide manhunt for the murders of Lloyd Eels, famous New York attorney, and his beautiful secretary, Meta Carson.'

Pop looked up, nodded sagely, and continued:

'The couple were murdered last Saturday night in Eels' New York apartment. Eels was shot and his body put in a closet in a vacant apartment next door. Miss Carson was brutally clubbed to death.

'The motive, police believe, was furnished by a document found in a locked safe in Eels' office. The document was an affidavit made by a woman named Mumsie McGonigle charging Bailey, whose real name is Peter Markham, with the murder of his partner, Jack Fisher, ten years ago.

'Fisher's body is buried in a meadow on the American River near Echo Pass, according to the affidavit. California authorities are en route to the spot –'

Caldwell got up, reached out and tore the paper from Pop's hands. He frowned down at the black print.

'I'll be a son of a bitch!' Caldwell said.

'Like I said,' the waitress yelled her two cents' worth. 'You could'a'knocked me over with a feather.'

'Didn't he ever make a pass at you?' asked Jack Wiles, who drove the Standard Oil truck between Bridgeport and Bishop.

'You go on,' the waitress said. 'He was a gentleman. Like I said – why, he was the last person you'd think of murdering people.'

'You never can tell,' Pop said.

Caldwell wasn't listening. He was reading the column after column of story about Red Bailey and all he could think of was Ann would be taking this hard. Jesus, it would be tough, people talking, people smirking at her, whispering, making out like they were sorry for her when they weren't – when they were pleased as all hell because this gave them something to talk about, something to fill out their stinking little lives.

At that moment he was sorry not only for Ann but for Bailey – the poor bastard having to kill because if he didn't he'd be hanged for something that happened a long time ago, the poor bastard running like a tired old buck toward the end of the hunting season. He hurled the paper on the floor.

'Shut up, for Christ's sake!' he roared and stamped out of the cafe.

'How do you like that?' Pop said, staring after him. 'Why – Why –'

'Me, I'd be cheering,' Wiles said. 'I'd be kicking up my heels and shooting off firecrackers if I was him.'

The waitress slapped the counter with her napkin. 'I think you're – why, I think you're awful. It just goes to show who has real feelings around here.'

'Speaking of real feelings, what are you doing tonight?' Wiles said, winking at her.

The waitress flounced back toward the kitchen, wiggling her hips.

Ann was lying face down by the creek at the west end on the Miller place when Caldwell found her. She was so still that for a minute he was afraid she was dead, lying there so close to the creek that the water just missed her feet.

He dropped down beside her, not saying anything, sorry

he had come. But he had been so damned worried, what with her running out of the house like that across the field, not paying any attention to her mother's yells. He had been afraid she would do something silly like trying to drown herself.

It was all right now. She was young and you got over things quickly when you were young. Anyway, it was just one of those things girls have for older men – sort of hero worship that never lasted. The thing to do was to act like nothing had happened, not to talk about it or scold her. That's what he told Canby and Mrs. Miller. He had talked turkey to them, straight-from-the-chest stuff. They were full of that I-told-you-so junk. Let him handle it. He was the one to do it because from now on that was his job, taking care of Ann.

He lighted a cigarette, leaned on one elbow and looked at the creek. The water was going down. He wished he had brought a rod along because they'd be biting good now, jumping right out of the water after a fly and he hadn't had time to fish for a week. Too much to do. Too many campers hanging around – people who hadn't been camping before and tried to get by without buying licenses.

Ann moved. Caldwell put a hand gently on her shoulder. 'Are you okay, kid?' he asked.

'Go away, please,' Ann said in a dead voice.

'You don't want to be alone,' Caldwell said. 'I'll just sit here and not talk.'

Ann sat up. In her eyes blazed a violence that frightened him. Then the look went away. She put her head in her hands and sighed. She said: 'Hello, Jimmy.'

'I was worried about you.'

'I'm all right.'

'Sure, you're all right.'

She dropped her hands and dug at the sand idly. 'Jimmy – there couldn't be –' She forced the words out – 'there couldn't be a mistake, could there?'

'I don't know,' Caldwell said.

'I want to go to him, Jimmy.'

Caldwell choked down a sudden flash of anger. He said softly, 'You can't do that, kid.'

She screamed at him. 'But they'll kill him. They'll find him and they'll kill him and I'll never see him again.' Then she was in his arms sobbing convulsively, digging her face into his shoulder. He kept patting her, saying, 'There, there, baby – there, there, baby.'

She stopped crying. Presently she pulled away from him and dabbed at her eyes. 'I'm sorry.'

'A good cry never hurt anyone,' Caldwell said.

'I guess I better go home.'

'No hurry. I saw your dad. He don't expect you today.'

She turned her face to him. 'I can't talk to them. They'll – they'll –'

'No, they won't. They won't say anything.'

Her hand went out, touched the back of his large brown one. 'Poor Jim. This isn't fair.'

'Don't you worry.'

'Jim. Do you think – maybe they won't catch him?'

'Maybe not.'

'And I'll bet – Jim, I'll bet he comes back here.'

Caldwell didn't look at her. He picked up a stone and tossed it into the creek. He might do it at that. Yes, sir, he might. That crazy red-headed bastard might do anything.

Automatically his fingers found his gun butt and felt the good roughness of it.

# CHAPTER FIFTEEN

THAT WEDNESDAY afternoon a Chevrolet coupe pulled up alongside the Ethyl pump. The driver got out and watched the Kid come across the yard from the grease rack. Not until the Kid was right in front of him did the man speak. Mouthing the words, he said, 'Ten ethyl and check the oil and water.'

The Kid went around to the pump and started running gas into the tank. The man followed him. He was very thin and tall and even when he smiled his face had a lugubrious expression. His name was Christopher Ryan and his unimaginative associates called him Slats.

'How's the fishing around here?' Slats asked, making sure the Kid's glance was fixed on his lips.

The Kid's vigorous nod indicated it was good.

Across the highway was an adobe motel. The cabins were fairly new, with a small restaurant at one end. Slats pointed to the motel. The Kid looked across the highway and back at him.

'Good place?' Slats asked.

Again the Kid nodded vigorously. He put the hose back on the pump, replaced the cap and moved forward to the hood of the car. He waited until Slats released the catch, then lifted the hood. Slats got back under the wheel. On the ledge back of the seat lay a new creel and a cardboard cylinder that held a fishing rod. Slats' khaki pants and shirt and his canvas hat were as new as the creel. A fishing license was pinned to the hatband.

The hood banged down. The Kid came to the side of the car and held out a hand. Slats put a five-dollar bill in it. When the Kid came back with the change, Slats gave him a fifty-cent tip. 'See you around,' Slats said.

The Kid grinned his thanks.

'Maybe you can show me where the fish are.'

Another grin, another nod. Slats put the car in gear, pulled away from the station and across the highway to the motel, got out in front of the manager's cabin and went inside. The Kid glanced after him, then returned to the Ford sedan suspended on the grease rack.

He had almost finished with the car when a white and black Mercury slid to a stop on the gravel and two men got out. One was a state copper. The other was the sheriff, Tom Douglas.

Douglas beckoned to the Kid who stood beside the rack looking at them with a blank, stupid expression. When he didn't answer the summons, Douglas went over to him and said with a smile, 'We want to talk to you.'

The Kid frowned and pointed to the station.

'Lock it up and come on,' Douglas said.

With a shake of his head the Kid refused.

'Now Kid,' Douglas pleaded. 'We just want to ask a few questions. Come on.'

'Shove the dumb son of a bitch into the car,' the state copper suggested.

Douglas ignored him. Douglas put one arm around the Kid's thin shoulders and piloted him toward the station. He pointed to the lock on the door and the locks on the pumps. The Kid hesitated, gave in, locked up the joint, followed Douglas over to the police car and got in back.

Sitting in the open doorway of one of the cabins Slats watched the police car head for the center of town. When it was out of sight, he sauntered across the highway and through the station to the white bungalow in back. After a while he reappeared, whistling softly to himself, and returned to his cabin.

The teletype started chattering when Douglas, the copper and the Kid came through the back door into the squad room of the State Highway Patrol office. Douglas and the state copper stopped by the machine and watched the keys printing black letters on the yellow paper. The Kid sat on a bench and awaited.

'Attn. Bridgeport,' the words marched across the paper. 'Bailey left plane Sacramento Sunday night. No trace. No record car sales Sacramento.'

The machine fell silent. Douglas and the state copper exchanged glances.

'He's headed this way, all right,' Douglas said. He started across the room toward the captain's office but the teletype suddenly came back to life, so he returned to it and watched the message take form.

'Attn. Bridgeport. Murder warrants en route. Skeleton uncovered in meadow near Strawberry. New York asks check on woman named Mumsie McGonigle. May be in your city.'

Douglas waited but there were no more messages. 'I don't get it,' he grumbled to himself. 'By Jesus, I don't get it.'

'Get what?' asked the state copper.

'Why in hell a New York attorney got himself mixed up in a California murder.'

The state copper gave Douglas a pitying look. 'This Fisher come from New York, didn't he?'

'Yes, but –'

'Bailey and Fisher was partners in New York, Tom. It adds up. Let's not worry about things making sense. Let's catch Bailey.'

'Let's,' said Douglas dryly, and taking the Kid by one arm he piloted him through a door.

Douglas was gentle with the Kid. He had two boys of his own – big, strapping fellows with nothing wrong with them except they wouldn't go to school, they hated work and they were on the make for every girl in the county. It seemed to him unfair that a nice, quite boy like the Kid, who wasn't afraid of work and who could catch fish where no one else could, should have to live in a soundless, speechless world. You had to hand it to the Kid, learning to read lips, learning to write, never getting sore at anyone. And what a loyal little bastard he was to Red! Douglas hated to ask him questions about Red, hated to sit there forming the questions simply and carefully so that the Kid's pale eyes could follow the movements of his lips. But he asked them and he didn't care much whether the Kid's written answers were lies or not.

No, the Kid hadn't seen Red. Last week he had a letter from him. Red was still in New York as far as he knew. His job was to take care of the station until Red came back and he wished they would get finished with him so he could go back to work.

Where was he yesterday? Fishing. Up the creek back of Twin Lakes.

Last night? The Kid wasn't home last night.

You know how it is when you get to fishing. You forget time. Then the car broke down and he had to fix it.

And the fish? Where were they?

The Kid scuffed the floor with his toe.

Well?

He sold them. To some guy in a Cadillac. And please don't say anything to Jim Caldwell, because it was against the law to sell fish. But the guy wanted them and the Kid was going to give them to him but he insisted on paying.

If he heard from Red, he'd tell them?

Of course. Only he didn't think Red killed anybody.

The state copper dropped him at the station then went on south to check on a smash-up. The Kid opened the station and started for the grease rack. Then he saw Ann Miller sitting on the steps of the bungalow staring straight ahead. He went over to her and squatted on the ground in front of her. She reached out and touched his hair.

107

With his forefinger the Kid wrote in the dust. 'They won't catch him.'

Ann tipped his head up. 'Where is he, Kid?'

Pale eyes scanned her face. Then the finger put an answer in the dust. 'I don't know.'

'You'd tell me?'

The Kid nodded. Again he wrote. 'Jim Caldwell.'

Ann sat up and looked around. The Kid pointed to the motel across the highway. There was a station wagon parked in front of the cafe.

'He wouldn't –' She didn't finish the sentence because she knew the answer. Jim Caldwell was watching her. Everyone in Bridgeport was watching her. She rose and started walking blindly down the highway. Ahead the peaks were golden and there were deep shadows in the canyons but she didn't see the hills, or the great meadow stretching away. The Kid watched her go. He sat down on the steps and put his head in his hands and cried a little.

Jim Caldwell came out of the cafe, leaned against the car and looked after the slim, lonely girl but he didn't follow.

In a rocker on the porch of a cabin down the line Slats sat rocking and smoking and thinking that with a dame like that around Red wouldn't be far off.


Guy Parker stood by the roulette table watching a fat woman put five-dollar chips on Number 23. When the number came up for the third time he dropped a handful of silver dollars on the number.

'For luck,' he said.

The little man standing behind the fat woman looked at Parker suspiciously and nudged her. The fat woman hesitated then pulled back all her chips but one. The ball skittered around the wheel, hesitated, dropped into 23. Parker pocketed his winnings, gave the fat woman a sad smile and went across the crowded noisy room and up the stairs.

Through the window at the end of the hall he could see the sky paling with dawn. He went to the window and let

108

the wind bring him the scent of honeysuckle. Like Mumsie, he thought, and turned back down the hall. Quietly he opened the door into his bedroom and crossed to the bed.

The bed was near the windows and the cool, half light showed her to him – one arm outstretched, the other at her side, her slim, full-breasted body sheathed in satin and lace. She had thrown the sheet aside.

It didn't matter to him that Mumsie was remote, or that there had been other men before him. He had her and he was going to keep her. When you put fifty grand on the line – or, rather, when you gave a guy that much of an interest in your gambling joint – for a dame like Mumsie, you kept your eyes open, you didn't miss a trick that might take her from you. Whit Sterling drove tough bargains and then treated you like he was God Almighty. The thought was like the feel of nettles against his skin.

Mumsie's long lashes lifted from her cheeks. She glanced past him toward the windows. 'Morning already?'

Parker sat on the edge of the bed and his thin fingers touched one breast.

'Coming to bed?'

'Pretty soon,' Guy said.

She yawned, snuggled her face into the pillow.

'Want me to?'

'Of course. You're sweet, Guy.'

Parker's mouth drew down in a smile. 'And generous.'

'Very.'

'That why you're here?'

Her eyes were closed. 'One reason.'

'What else?'

'I said you were sweet.'

He couldn't tell from her tone whether she meant it or not. Nor did it seem to him incongruous to be labeled that. She had a good life, all the dough she wanted, all the clothes she wanted. No illusions. He looked at the whole business realistically. Mumsie once shot a guy to get dough. She ran out on another to keep it. But she wouldn't shoot him and

109

she wouldn't run out on him. He kissed the breast, pushed back her pale hair, rose and went into the hall.

Joe Stefanos was coming up the stairs. Parker waited for him outside the sitting room.

'Get some sleep?' Parker asked.

'Sure.' Stefanos opened the door, crossed to the leather armchair, dropped in it and stretched. 'Did you give her a kiss for me?'

Parker closed the door. 'I catch you around her, you'll be looking at the world from the bottom of Pyramid Lake.'

Stefanos was not impressed. 'She sure got her hooks in you.'

The remark amused Parker. He was still grinning as he came from the desk to where Joe was sitting and dropped an envelope in his lap, 'Get on your horse.'

Joe felt the thinness of the plain white envelope. 'A stall?'

'I know what I'm doing.'

'So do I – know what you're doing.' Stefanos stretched again.

'Also I know why.'

'A man can be too goddamned smart.'

'That's the way I look at it.' His round bug eyes regarded Parker without fear. 'You, for instance. You ain't got a chance to screw Whit, Guy.'

'No? Who said I was going to?'

'Me.'

'Run and tell him.'

'I ever double-cross you?'

'Don't start.'

'All I got to say is, you try to screw him and we all get in a mess. She ain't worth it, Guy.'

'What do you mean?' Parker said sharply.

Imperturbably Stefanos went on: 'You figure Whit will make a deal with Red and she'll be part of the deal – ain't that it?'

Parker moved to the window and stared moodily out. Daylight was coming quickly.

'But you get your mitts on that file, then he can't put a frame around her.'

'Or you,' Parker added, turning.

Stefanos got up and tapped the arm of the chair with the envelope. His face was drawn and his eyes seemed more proturberant than ever. 'You ain't worrying about me. Only her.'

'Who would you worry about?'

'Her. But she ain't worth it.'

'You'll get your cut and you'll live to spend it.'

Stefanos laughed and the sound of the laugh wasn't pleasant. He went out and slammed the door.


Another car was in the station when the Dodge pulled up beside the pump. The Kid was wiping the windshield. It was an old sedan and there were a bedspring and mattress strapped to the top. Four kids were in the back seat and a tired man and woman in the front seat. The car pulled over in front of the restrooms and the kids piled out. The little Greek told the Kid to put in ten gallons. Then he got out and bent down beside the right rear tire. When the Kid went past he slipped him the envelope.

Straightening, the little Greek watched the Kid pump gas into the tank. He sauntered over to the fountain and had a drink. He glanced across the street. Slats was sitting on the front porch. The Greek stretched, gave the Kid two dollars, got in and drove around the motel and up the highway.

Slats saw Joe's car but he gave no sign of recognition. Slats rocked and watched the station and waited. Cars kept coming in and the Kid kept right on pumping gas. Presently Slats went inside and lay on the bed. Through the window he could keep an eye on the Kid.

An hour passed. The Kid locked up the pumps and the door, went on the back to the cottage and entered. Slats got off the bed. Soon the Kid came out with an old creel slung across one shoulder and a rod in one hand, opened the

111

garage, backed the Ford roadster out and drove north along the highway.

A door led from the cabin into the garage. Slats tossed his rod and creel into the car, sat smoking for five minutes then headed up the highway after the Kid. He drove slowly, keeping a wary eye ahead of him because he didn't want to pass the roadster. When he sighted it he cut his speed more and kept about a quarter of a mile between the two cars. There were long, open stretches of road and every so often he caught a glimpse of the roadster plugging on ahead.

A state police car cruised past and disappeared around a bend. Slats wondered if they had the same idea he had. That would muss up the deal. It sure would. But when Slats topped a rise, there was the Kid's car down at the foot of the hill and the police car was out of sight. Slats' foot sought the brake and his car moved slower. The Kid's car went around a curve and a hill was between Slats and the other.

Beyond the curve a dirt road forked left and wandered off toward the mountains. Dust hung over the road and yonder it boiled up to mark the passage of an automobile. Slats stopped, got out and saw the print of tires leading off. A metal sign, pocked by bullets from the guns of frustrated deer hunters, said the road led to Elm Creek.

Now Slats didn't have to hold his coupe back. The dirt road did that. It was bad and the dust was inches deep. He hung to the wheel, swallowed dust and wished he was at the corner of Forty-Second Street and Broadway. The brush thinned out. A pine forest climbed the hill and the road climbed with it, then snaked down into a canyon where a line of alders marked a creek. A shaky wooden bridge rattled under his wheels and he was almost past the Kid's car before he saw if half hidden in an alder thicket.

Slats drove on a way, pulled off into some pines, got out and, carrying his rod and creel, walked cautiously back to the bridge. A path led down to the stream and there were footprints on the path. The footprints crossed a strip of wet sand and went on up the creek. Slats put his rod together and threaded his line. With expert fingers he tied a leader on and put a coachman and a gray hackle on the leader. He made a few tentative casts. With satisfied surprise he felt a sudden strike. He flicked his wrist, setting the hook, then played the trout until it tired. He reeled it in. A good one. Half a pound at least. He opened his creel and dropped it on top of two forty-five automatics. He started upstream after the Kid.

Three quarters of an hour later, when the Kid crept cautiously downhill through the forest toward the road, he found two cars screened by the trees – a black and white Mercury was hidden two hundred yards from the bridge. Fifty yards beyond was the Chevrolet. The Kid ran down the road, backed his Ford out and drove hurriedly away.

Darkness filled the canyon when he reached Red's camp. Red poured him a drink of Scotch and filled the tin cup with water from the bucket outside the tent. He opened the envelope and read Guy Parker's brief note. Whit Sterling, it appeared, was in the back country fishing for a few days. Guy was sending a man in after him. Guy was sure that Whit would see him. Guy said to sit tight.

Red handed the letter over to the Kid. 'They're stalling,' he said.

The Kid read it, nodded, grinned. Then his nimble fingers started talking and as they formed letters the Kid chuckled and his blue eyes danced.

# CHAPTER SIXTEEN

MILLER LOOKED up from his newspaper and watched Ann with troubled eyes. Across the breakfast table, Mrs. Miller dug into a stack of hot cakes, put a forkful of food in her mouth and kept right on reading the comic page. She paid no attention to her husband when he rose and went over to the sideboard where Ann was making sandwiches.

'Kind of lonesome at the office these days,' Miller said, letting his hand rest on her shoulder.

Ann didn't speak. She spread butter thinly on the white bread and put bits of meat and lettuce on top of the butter.

'Going fishing again?'

Ann nodded. She wrapped the sandwich in waxed paper and put it in the creel that stood on the sideboard.

'Jimmy going along?' His tone was hopeful.

'No,' Ann said.

'Jimmy's a fine boy.' The comment brought no response. Miller fumbled in his mind, said, 'He's having a rough time of it.'

'Yes, dad.' She put the second sandwich in the creel, slung it over one shoulder and held her face up for his kiss that found a ghost of a smile. She picked up her rod that leaned against the wall near the back door and pushed the door open. Mrs. Miller looked up from the paper, and started to put some of her bitter disapproval into words. But Miller's sharp glance killed the unborn speech.

The screen door slammed. They watched her cross the

yard to the sagging gate and follow the trail a thousand hooves had cut deep in the meadow grass.

'She's going to meet him,' Mrs. Miller said. 'You know it and you do nothing to stop her.'

'Let her alone,' he said. He slammed the door as he entered the living room.

Mrs. Miller looked after him, her thin lips forming words but the words were for herself and remained unspoken. Then she sighed and went back to her reading, finding solace in the bloodthirsty antics of her favorite comic characters.

In the rocky waste back of the mountain wall the wind found a few clouds and herded them across the sky, as though displeased with its pale blue emptiness. A covey of quail whirred out of a willow clump, to cross Ann's path. In the pasture beyond the creek a lark gave sudden thanks for morning. The creek meandered lazily over to the highway, gathered strength to plunge through the culvert, then placidly continued through the broad, pleasant pastures where the silly sheep nibbled aimlessly at the sweet grass.

Gradually the bit of world Ann knew so well gave her some of its brightness. He was alive and he was somewhere near at hand. Soon she would find him – lying beside the creek, waiting for her in some tiny hidden meadow ringed with lodgepole pine. So thinking, and knowing again quick thrusts of happiness, she put her rod together, threaded the line through the eyelets, tied her leader on the line and began tempting the wary German Brown and even warier Lochleven with two bright-feathered tufts.

By noon a ridge was between her and the broad meadow and the voice of the creek was louder as it found its way through a narrow canyon. She discovered a stretch of sand behind a rock, put her fishing basket in the shade and climbed the rock. She looked up and down the canyon. Below her the creek paused long enough to form a pool before it hurried on. The water in the rocky pool was deep and cold. She jumped down, stripped off her clothes and let her body slide into the green depths, holding her breath as the cold fingers tugged at her. She swam across and back to scramble up and know again the good warmth of sand and sun and wind.

For a while she lay face down on the sand, her eyes closed, her mind dulled by the warmth the sun spilled into the narrow gorge. Yet she found, now and then, some memory of him to savor and cherish. A moment on a hill top. His tall strong body swinging along a trail. The pungent scent of sundrenched bear clover and pine needles all around them. Life would be good again and life would be full and rich again. She heard the promise in the rush of water through the tortuous rocky passage, in the singing of the wind through the pines straggling up the steep and stony hillside. Then a voice pushed itself into her consciousness.

'A water baby,' the voice said.

She threw a startled glance upward. A thin, khaki-clad fisherman stood on the rock looking down at her.

Her quick hand found her clothes and pulled them over her. 'Go away,' she said.

'I like it here.'

'Please. Let me dress.'

The man dropped down on the rock and let his legs dangle. Deftly he rolled a cigarette, lighted it and grinned at her. 'Fish don't bite good around noon, do they?'

An evil face, she thought, desperately tucking her scant clothing about her – a thin, hard cruel face. And the voice, despite its softness, evil. Hungrily his glance swept over her and she shuddered. Slimy and cold. Like brushing against a water dog as you swam across a stagnant pool.

'Waiting for someone?' he asked.

Automatically she started to say no, then hoping that a lie would send him on his way she said hurriedly, 'Yes, I am. He'll be here very soon.'

'That'll be nice,' the man said, not moving, dribbling smoke from his nostrils. He brought his fishing basket closer and opened the lid.

116

'Go away,' she repeated. 'Please go away.'

He took something from the basket and slid it in his pocket but his body shielded the object. As he started down the rock she jumped up and tried to scramble away from him. A hand caught her shoulder. She threw it off and plunged into the pool, swam over behind the shelter of a boulder and, gripping the slippery stone, hurled broken, frightened phrases at him. He stood on the sand, grinning now at her, now at her clothing crumpled at his feet.

'Kind of cold, ain't it?' he asked. Because he was watching her, and because the sound of the creek echoed all around him, he did not see the Kid clamber down behind him, did not hear the crunch of the Kid's footsteps on the sand.

The Kid had a rock in one hand. He swung the rock and slammed it against the man's head. The slat-like body folded and he went down on his hands and knees, trying desperately to stay conscious, trying to push darkness back so he could see his attacker. There was sand in his eyes and sand in his mouth and the canyon tumbled in on him.

When he pushed himself up and saw the canyon walls again and the dark water swirling around the shining stones, he was alone on the little strip of sand. Painfully he pulled himself up on the rock. Nothing moved but the water and the wind-racked trees. The sun was sliding down the sky and somewhere far up the canyon thunder muttered faintly.

'That red bastard!' he said aloud, at last finding anger for his quarry, finding a reason other than an order for killing him. He transferred some of the anger toward himself. What a goddamned fool. One look at a naked dame and he let the guy he was looking for sneak up behind him and knock his brains out. The memory of Ann's brown body gave him no pleasure because knives of pain stabbed at his skull. Nausea made him dizzy. He crouched on the boulder, retching and cursing.

Beyond the ridge Ann swung lithely down the trail. Close behind her was the Kid. Now and then he stopped to look

117

back, keeping one hand at his waistband where the butt of one of Slat's forty-fives protruded.

When they reached the flat land and climbed through the fence to the sheltering wall of willows, Ann stopped to rest. The Kid came up and squatted beside her at the edge of the creek.

'Thanks, Kid.' Ann patted his skinny shoulder.

The Kid shook his head and his lips smiled but his eyes didn't. Desperate anger lay in them, an anger at the wall of silence that would never be broken down.

Her fingers dug into his shoulder. 'Such a good boy,' she said softly.

The Kid's throat tightened as though the million words that could never be spoken were rising up to choke him. For a moment tears clouded the pale blue of his eyes. He shook his head, clearing the angry frustration from his mind. One finger put words on the wet sand. 'I should have killed him.'

'No, Kid.'

The Kid's thin hand smoothed the sand. The Kid smiled at her, stood up and helped her to her feet. North, a thin column of smoke was a monument to some hill fire and already the sun flushed angrily. The Kid looked at the smoke for a moment, then led her across the lush pasture toward her home. He carried baskets and rods and when they reached the fence he squeezed her hand, gave her her things and hurried off toward the highway. She watched him go, thinking, *Poor Kid! Poor, silent, tortured Kid*, wanting to hold him close, because she knew that's what he wanted, that's what he would always want and never could have.

Jim Caldwell's station wagon stood in the yard in the shade of the poplars. Jim was in the kitchen drinking coffee and eating hot doughnuts as Mrs. Miller dipped them from the pot of grease.

'Any luck?' Jim said, getting up and following her to the sink, a half eaten doughnut in one hand and a coffee cup in the other.

118

'Some.' Ann pulled wet fern from the basket, spilled the shining bodies of the trout into the sink.

'Good ones,' Jim said admiringly. 'Maybe I better weigh 'em up. Maybe you got more than the limit there.' He drained the cup, licked the crumbs from his fingers. 'They started work today.'

She turned a puzzled glance on him.

'Up at my new place,' Jim said. 'It's going to be swell.'

She found a warm smile for him, aching because that was so little to give a man with so much love shining in his eyes.

Red Bailey's service station was locked up tight, so the little Greek drove on through town to the Sierra Bar, parked his Dodge around back and went inside. The bar was across the street from the highway patrol station and a couple of state coppers were drinking beer and kidding the big-hipped broad who was waiting on table. Joe slid up on a stool near the table where the state coppers were and told the guy dishing out the booze to give him a rye old-fashioned. He sipped it and listened to the cops telling the broad not to forget to stick around after midnight. He gave her the once-over out of the corner of one eye and wondered what the hell anyone would want with her. She said she'd be there ready and willing and went on her way. Then the cops started talking about Red Bailey so Joe hunched over the bar and tried not to appear interested.

The boys, it seemed, had been looking all over for Red, but hell, how could you find a guy who knew those hills like he did if he was hiding out up there? Anyway somebody had seen Red in Reno and somebody else had seen him in Fresno and somebody else had seen him in L.A., and if you had the law on your tail would you be sap enough to stick your neck out where everybody knew you?

Joe had a couple more old-fashioneds. By that time the cops had made themselves scarce. He went on through the arch into the cafe, ordered a steak, French frieds and coffee and read about Red Bailey while he ate. Things were cooling off. The guy who wrote the story tried to get all steamed up but there wasn't much to be steamed up about. They hadn't found him and they were still looking and that was that. He looked up to see Slats coming in. Slats went past him to the counter. His hat was pulled down but you could see the patch of bandage on the side of his head.

Joe went back to the paper, eating slowly and sending an occasional cold look from his frog eyes at Slats' back. A dame with a scrawny neck took Joe's plate away and shoved a menu in front of him. Joe ordered apple pie a la mode and another cup of coffee. By the time he finished Slats was on his way out. Joe waited a couple of minutes and then went out and drove his Dodge down beyond the motel, parked it well off the highway and walked back to Slats' dark cabin.

At his knock Slats opened the door a crack, saw who it was and let him in. He pulled down the shade and switched on the light.

'Who slugged you?' Joe asked.

'A rock.' Slats dug a bottle of Scotch out of his bag, got a couple of glasses and fixed drinks for them. 'I was fishing and I slipped on a wet rock. Damn near drowned.'

'And so you didn't find Red,' said Joe dryly.

'Not yet. I will.'

'We ain't got all year.'

'You want to take over?' Slats emptied his glass and spilled more Scotch in it. 'I got a slippery dummy and a dame to watch.'

'Never mind the dame. Just the Kid,' Joe said. He took a folded paper from a pocket and handed it to Slats.

Slats read it. It was from Red and it told Guy Parker to quit stalling. It told Guy to get hold of Whit Sterling right away.

'That was mailed from here last night,' said Joe. 'So the dummy saw him yesterday. Where were you?'

'Little son of a bitch ditched me.'

'He wise?'

'No. The cops were tailing him and he pulled a fast one on them and I got sucked in.'

'And today?'

'I tailed the dame. No luck.'

'She didn't slug you with the rock?'

Slats dropped his lids to hide the anger in his eyes. 'No. I think maybe I know where to look for him now.'

'Yeah?'

'Up where she went fishing.'

Joe's laugh mocked him. 'Red ain't that nuts – to tell a dame where he is.' He got up, took an envelope from one pocket and pitched it on the bed. 'Slide that under the service station door late tonight. Tomorrow don't let the dummy shake you.'

Gingerly Slats touched the bandage back of his ear. 'Not me. One for the road?' He held out the bottle.

'Sure.' Joe had a drink then let himself through the door into the garage and went around back of the motel toward his car.

Slats had three more stiff drinks. It was midnight so he switched off the lights and crossed the highway to the dark station and slid the envelope under the door. The drinks stirred up the anger in him but they also stirred up the memory of naked, sun-tanned skin on clean white sand. Maybe with Red out of the way a guy could get some of that. Anyway, a guy could have a stab at it.

# CHAPTER SEVENTEEN

AT THREE O'CLOCK the following afternoon the Kid filled the Ford roadster with gas, locked the station and drove east through town, then south where the highway turned. Slats was watching from his cabin window and when the Ford was out of sight he came out on the porch, to lounge there. Thunderheads were rising behind the hills and the wind was pushing them out over the valley. The air was heavy with the threat of rain.

Presently a black and white Mercury pulled out from behind the state highway patrol office and headed leisurely in the same direction the Kid had taken. Slats went back into the cabin, made a highball and returned to the rocker on the porch. Yes, sir, he had the dummy figured out this time. He'd be back after he ditched the cops.

Two other men watched the Kid's car until it was out of sight. One was the sheriff, Tom Douglas, and the other was Jim Caldwell. They sat by the two-way radio in the highway patrol office and through the big window they saw the Kid's car go by and a few minutes later saw the Mercury take after it.

'I hope they took their fishing rods along,' Jim said, as the black and white car went on through the town and turned south. 'Because all they're gonna catch is fish.'

Douglas brooded over his pipe. 'Maybe not, Jim.'

'What's Red want to see the Kid for?'

Douglas shrugged. 'We don't want to miss no bets.'

122

'Red ain't nobody's fool,' Jim admitted grudgingly. 'You had the law on your tail, would you let a guy working for you come up to visit?'

'You don't think Red came back here then?'

Caldwell shook his head. 'Oh, he'll come back. Sure. And when he does I'll know about it.'

The sheriff raised his thick eyebrows enquiringly. 'You will?'

'Yeah?'

'How?'

Jim's lips didn't answer but his mind did. How? A girl's eyes would tell him. That's what he was waiting for. A look. A shining softness that wasn't there now. The thought made anger flame inside him. One of these days he'd see that look and then he would follow her and that would be the end of Red Bailey. Oh, he'd play it smart. He wouldn't be in on the finish. Let Tom or one of the state coppers handle that end because he wanted Ann. She wouldn't know. He'd wait a day or so after it happened and then he'd drop around and not say much and let things ride along. Go hunting with her maybe. Take her out and show her his new place and pretty soon she'd forget that ugly bastard.

Douglas was watching him. He read the answer to his question in Jim's eyes so he let the matter drop. Jim got up, buttoned his coat and put on his Stetson.

'Stick around,' Douglas suggested.

'Waste of time,' said Jim. 'Anyway I got to go up to Twin Lakes. Some guy shot a couple of doe.'

'Whyn't you ask Ann to go?' The sheriff asked kindly. He liked Ann and he liked Jim and he wanted to see them get together.

Jim started to tell him to mind his own business, saw kindness in the other's expression and went off without speaking. Douglas watched him cross the highway to where the station wagon was parked by the Sierra Bar, thinking, Jim's probably right. The Kid isn't the one we should be watching.

123

He settled back, filled his pipe and waited, seeing cloud shadows sweep across the far meadows, hearing the distant growl of thunder and getting no satisfaction from the imminence of a storm – to him usually soul-stirring.

A door behind him opened and the captain came through to fiddle with the radio dials and announce that it sure looked like rain. Douglas puffed at his pipe and agreed that it did.

'My boys are all set,' the captain said.

'Mine too.'

'Where's Jim?'

'Went up to Twin Lakes.'

'He don't want to be in on the kill?'

'Says there won't be any kill today,' Douglas replied. 'I think maybe he's right.'

The radio interrupted them. A droning voice filled the little room.

'Calling KYBZ,' the voice said. 'Come in KYBZ.'

The captain flipped a switch with eager fingers. 'KYBZ,' he said. 'KYBZ.'

'This is Kelly,' the droning voice from the speaker said. 'The Kid's car turned off at Bryce Creek. Shall we follow?'

'Wait there,' the captain said.

The radio was silent. Douglas knocked the dottle from his pipe and stood up. 'We'll come in from the back above the falls. You follow the creek up.'

The captain nodded and disappeared through the door into the squad room. As the sheriff walked toward his office the captain's car pulled out along the highway. A moment later another car flanked by two motorcycle cops followed.

Four deputies were waiting on the porch of Douglas' office. He motioned to a waiting sedan. They piled in and he got in front with the driver.

'Want the siren?' the driver asked.

Douglas gave him a disgusted look and settled back against the cushion. Rain drops splashed against the windshield. Then the sun came out again as the wind tore the clouds to bits and drove them east.

*

124

The Bryce Creek road was oiled. It snaked through heavy timber up a narrow valley to cross Bryce Greek ten miles from the highway. The Kid didn't get that far. A mile from the forks he pulled off the road and bumped along a cow trail into a pine thicket. He got out of the car and lay in a patch of bear clover watching the road. He didn't have long to wait. Within half an hour two motorcycles came around the bend. Behind them came the two Mercurys and the Buick. The Kid gave them ten minutes' start. Then he drove out to the road and high-tailed it for Bridgeport, warily watching the rear-view mirror. When he went through the town he made sure there were no cops following him.

Slats was on the porch and when the Kid's car turned north he went slowly into the cabin, stopped long enough for a quick one, then entered the garage and slid under the wheel. Those cops were going to be plenty sore, letting themselves get sucked out of the play. That dummy was a smart little son of a bitch. Only he wasn't quite smart enough. Slats grinned and put his car in gear.

It was a pipe to follow the dummy. He barreled along around fifty. Slats kept enough distance between the two cars so the dummy wouldn't spot him. Slats was plenty careful because this time had to be it. Maybe he stayed closer than he should but he didn't want to find himself chasing nothing. The thought of the cops tailing each other to hell-and-gone put a pleased grin on his thin, bony face. Well, maybe when he got through with Red they could have him. Unless Guy Parker wanted Red clean out of the picture.

Ahead, the Ford was slowing for a turn. The dummy stuck his hand out and swung the car across and along another highway leading west. Slats slowed down until the Ford was out of sight. Then noting the sign that said this was the Sonora Pass road, he followed, keeping his speed down to twenty-five, watching the road on either side. Across the river he spotted a dirty tent pitched in a little meadow. He put on the brake and looked all around for the dummy's car. When he didn't see it he drove on.

The road followed the river, climbing gradually upward. Through the pines you could see snow lying on the granite shoulders of the mountains. Slats pushed the throttle down and now he wasn't smiling. Lost him, he thought, as the mileposts drifted by and there was no sign of the Ford and no sign of a road leading off – only the unbroken forest and the river roaring down.

He almost missed it. He rounded a sharp turn and was past an opening in the trees when the flash of sun on metal told him where the dummy had hidden his car. He backed up and could see a black fender. He pulled off the highway and drove over rocks and brush and there it was and the dummy nowhere around. He couldn't see the river but he could hear it roaring down a gorge.

Carefully he walked forward, rod in one hand, his other hand thrust into the fishing basket. A faint trail angled down for a way and where there were no pine needles he saw new footprints. He stopped suddenly for the trail reached the lip of the gorge. Down below was the river and standing on a rock was the dummy. He had a short casting rod in his right hand. Now and then he reeled in and cast, with the flash of metal as the spinner shot across into a deep pool.

Slats drew back, dropped on his hands and knees and crawled forward. He lay face down when he reached the gorge's edge and scanned the winding river's course – first west, then east. She was sure a rough son of a bitch up here. A guy had to watch his step or he'd find himself bumping around the rocks.

No sign of Red. No sign of anyone but the dummy. After a bit the Kid reeled in and clambered over the rocks to disappear with the river where the gorge turned sharply. Slats went after him.

The water boiled against the boulders, roaring down and down, hesitating in the big potholes to cut away another grain of granite. It spilled out over smooth, shining slabs, down into other potholes. Slats reached the bend, moving cautiously, hiding himself behind boulders, hiding himself in crevices. Carefully he pulled himself up a boulder and peered ahead to find that the river snaked suddenly around another bend. No dummy. He must have cut over the hill. Slats pulled himself to the top of the boulder.

He was used to heights and he was used to roaring streams but as he looked down at the turbulent, angry river trying desperately to rip its stone bed apart, he felt a sudden dizziness. At that moment the thought of finding Red Bailey seemed a little foolish. Here he was risking his neck and when he got Red all he'd have would be the satisfaction of seeing a guy die – and a couple of bucks. To hell with it! But there was Lou and there was Parker and there was Stefanos and maybe the river was easier to take. He steadied himself then started along the rock.

He saw it coming. He saw the bright bit of metal before it hit him. He saw wet line arching away. But he was not quick enough. The spinner's hooks bit through his shirt into his chest and he felt the barbs sink in as the line went taut. He pitched forward and saw the river coming up to meet him.

The Kid watched the wild water shake Slats' body, slam it against rocks, carry it down to leave it in a pothole. He stood on a ledge below the boulder on which Slats had stood, holding his casting rod in one hand while with the other he hung on to a sapling. The singing reel, which he had never heard and which he would never hear, was silent. He kept jerking the rod and the spinner came free. He reeled in his line and went slowly up the cliff, stopping only once to rest, not looking back because there was no need to.

# CHAPTER EIGHTEEN

GUY PARKER didn't see him when he opened the door. Dawn was beyond the windows, too busy getting rid of night to bother with the darkness cloaking Guy's sitting room.

From the driveway below came the hum of departing motors, the whisper of tires on gravel, the unintelligible mutter of tired voices. Guy closed the door, flicked on the lights and was halfway across the room before he noticed Red sitting in the armchair. Red had a gun in one hand.

'Pull up a chair,' Red said, motioning with the long-barrelled thirty-eight.

A momentary look of surprise showed in Guy's face and the skin seemed to tighten across his bony cheeks. Then the tired, gray mask fell into place again. He said, 'Hello Red.' He pulled a straight-backed chair over and straddled it, leaning on the back.

'Good morning,' Red said.

'Little risky showing your puss around here, don't you think?'

'You worried about me?'

Red rose, went over to the door and locked it. He poured himself a drink from the Scotch bottle on the sideboard. 'Mix you one?'

'No, thanks.'

'Your man fell in the West Walker yesterday.' Red brought the drink back to the chair, sprawled back against the leather.

'And don't ask what man, because you know his name and I don't.'

Guy yawned. 'Jesus, I'm tired. Everybody and his brother showed up last night.'

'I was wrong,' Red said.

'Yes?'

'All these years I've been thinking you were smart. You're not.'

'I'm not the one the cops are after.'

'I wasn't thinking of cops. I was thinking of Whit Sterling. He's a man who nurses a grudge, Guy. Take me. Ten years he nursed a grudge. Think he'd make an exception in your case?'

'I'm not crossing him.'

'That's right.' Red grinned. 'So let's go see him.'

'Goddamn it, Red,' Guy said. He managed to sound annoyed, put out about the whole business. 'You got my note, didn't you? He's still in the back country.'

'And you sent one of your boys after him.'

'Yes.'

'Like hell. You sent one of your boys after me. He got carless and fell in the river.'

'He was just —'

Red's cruel grin cut Guy's speech in two.

'We haven't much time,' Red said. 'The cops are much smarter than me or you. I know the hills but they know them too. They'll catch up to me one of these days. Then I'll have to talk fast and you'll be in the soup with Whit and Whit'll be in the soup with the Treasury Department. I don't mind taking the rap for Jack Fisher but I won't take the credit for Eels or Meta Carson.'

'What good can Whit do you?' Guy didn't look at Red.

'You're not smart but you're smart enough to figure that out.'

Guy studied the rug. Guy asked in a toneless voice: 'You're willing to take the Fisher rap?'

129

Red drained his glass before he spoke. 'I'm not making deals. I don't have to.'

Guy's strong hands gripped the chair back and the wood cracked. 'You killed him,' he said fiercely. 'Goddamn it, you killed him.'

'We were wrestling,' Red said.

'Then what are you worried about? You can claim self-defense. You can get off maybe with a manslaughter rap.' No hiding of emotions now. The man was pleading with Red and Red knew it. Red was not impressed.

'You don't have to look close to see the frame,' Red chided. 'It's such a beautiful big one.'

'Is that what's worrying you?'

'Don't speak of it so lightly,' Red replied. 'You're not in it, Guy.'

'Can I get myself a drink?'

Red handed him his empty glass. 'One for me. And don't ring any bells.'

Parker came back with two highballs, gave Red one and started walking up and down, talking rapidly, trying to hide his emotion with quick bursts of words. They could work together. Together they were a match for Whit Sterling, for any son of a bitch in the world. Both of them would come out of it with a fistful of dough. Stefanos killed Eels and Meta Carson. They'd give Stefanos to the cops.

Red listened and Red did some figuring. The thing that had puzzled him didn't puzzle him any more. When Guy finally stopped talking Red asked in a quiet voice, 'Is she worth it, Guy?'

Guy didn't ask whom he meant. Guy didn't answer the question.

Red put his empty glass on the carpet by the chair. 'You're taking a hell of a risk for a dame. Whit. The Greek.'

'We've got Whit where we want him. I'll manage Joe.'

'We?'

'You then.'

'And I'm a man who lets bygones be bygones.'

130

'I had to do it.' Guy stood over him, confused and beaten. 'You know that, Red. Whit said –'

'And now you ask Whit to jump through hoops?'

'I had nothing to him then.'

'You've nothing on him now,' said Red. 'You've nothing on anyone. You're just a blowedup sucker. An ex-copper with a yen.'

Guy found some courage then. Guy said, 'I know one thing. Where Whit is. You can't play it alone.'

'I could try.'

'You sure could. You could tell the truth – and who in hell would believe you?'

'The Treasury boys.'

'But not the cops,' Guy said. 'I know how cops feel about things.'

'Do cops feel?'

'You killed one man. Don't forget that.'

Red stood up. 'Maybe you're right. Let's go.'

'A deal?' Guy held out a hand.

Red took it, smiled, pocketed his gun and followed the other into the hall and along it to the narrow stairway that would let them out the back way. Behind them a door opened so quietly they did not hear it, so they didn't see Mumsie's serene face framed in the narrow opening.

From the summit you could see Tahoe far below – the whole blue waste of it sleeping in the sun. Hills walled it in, walled in the broad meadows to the south. Here and there like teardrops were other tiny lakes. As always, when he looked down on the big lake, he felt his spirits lift. You didn't amount to anything and what happened to you didn't matter. He glanced over at Guy, brooding over the wheel of the Cadillac and said, 'Do you ever mourn for the wasted years?'

'For Christ's sake!' Guy said, turning his attention momentarily from the winding road.

'If I'm hanged I'd like to be hanged from a sugar pine,' Red said. 'A good high one.'

131

'Let's not talk about hanging.' Expertly Guy sent the car down the long grade. 'We miss a trick, we won't hang anyway.'

'How did you happen to get mixed up with Mumsie, Guy?'

'Who said I was mixed up with her.'

'I was going to show her Tahoe once,' Red said, ignoring the question. 'From the top of Echo Pass. Only she skipped out on me while I was digging a grave.'

'Jesus, you're cheerful this morning.'

'It's the altitude. So I had to look at it alone that time. It was just as well. I don't think Mumsie cares much about lakes. Was the dough all gone when you ran into her?'

'Quit worrying that bone.'

'Was it?'

'What do you care?'

'There are blank pages in the book. I'd like to fill them in. Mumsie's mixed up in my life too.'

'You still want her?' Guy asked sharply.

Red shook his head. 'My interest is objective. I did a lot of wondering about her the past ten years. You get over Mumsie but you remain curious. An impersonal curiosity.'

'You don't get over her.' Guy was suddenly intense. 'You're a damned liar when you say you get over her.'

'I did. She's haunting me now but that's your fault. So the least you can do is fill in the blanks.'

A Shell oil truck crawled down ahead of them. Guy waited for a straight stretch of road, swung around the truck and drove for a mile or so before he spoke. It was as though he brought up bits of the past to reassure himself, to convince himself that he could not lose her. 'She was putting dimes on number fourteen at a wheel in the Sky Club in Reno,' Guy said. 'I was running the wheel. I let her win.'

'And next night she came back?'

'And the night after that. I kept letting her win. We got to going around together. One night she was playing and then she ducked out. Whit Sterling came over to the table and dropped a buck on the red and started asking questions about her. I did some figuring. So we moved down to Las Vegas.'

'But you didn't shake Whit.'

'No. We didn't shake him.'

'One never does, apparently,' said Red.

'I had some dough,' Guy went on. 'I was looking around for a spot and I found it. I opened my own joint. One night there was Whit walking in the door. We went upstairs and had a talk and he didn't bother us any more.'

'How much?'

'How much what?'

'Did it cost you?'

'Who said it cost me anything?'

'I'm a realist, Guy. Whit's a realist, Hell, we're all realists. Particularly Mumsie. So you gave him a piece of your joint and one day he dropped by and said there's a red bastard running a service station down at Bridgeport. Mumsie knows all about him and maybe you can find out something that would be useful.'

'Something like that,' Guy agreed.

'Did it take much persuasion? To make her talk?'

'It's a nice day,' Guy said.

'Now, now. Feed my ego, will you? I'd like to think you used a rubber hose or a lighted cigarette.'

'I didn't.'

'I'm cut to the quick,' Red said. He yawned, settled back and gave his attention to the forest and to the glimpses of blue water through the trees.

The big stone house stood on a shoulder of the hill back of Emerald Bay. From the porch you could see most of the lake, the color changing from dark green to blue, then to a lighter shade of blue. Iron gates barred the graveled road leading from the highway. It took two blasts of the horn to bring a man down to open the gates. He gave Guy the once-over, his expression of cold disinterest not changing when he recognized the gambler. The gates swung open and the

133

Cadillac climbed the twisting drive to come to a halt under the porte-cochere.

'He lives well,' Red said, getting out and appraising the two-story structure of flat fieldstone and redwood. 'I remember something about the wages of sin.'

'Since when was gambling a sin?' asked Guy.

'I was thinking of his allied enterprises.'

'There's no dough in whores any more,' Guy said.

It wasn't necessary to ring the bell. The side door opened when they reached it and a dignified old fellow with a bit of an accent said, 'Good morning Mr. Parker.' He ushered them into a long, redwood-paneled room that looked out on the lake through big windows. A small fire burned in the massive fireplace, though the morning was not cold. The good smell of the pine smoke sharpened the soft wind coming from the lake. Whit Sterling was digging into a Persian melon at a table near the windows. He said, without looking up, 'It's been a long time, Red.'

Red dropped into the chair at the table facing him. 'Ten years.'

'Nine.'

'I wasn't counting that exchange of pleasantries in front of the Biltmore.'

'I'd rather think of that time,' Whit said. 'I want to enjoy my breakfast. Have you eaten?'

Red shook his head, Whit pushed a button with his foot and the man who had met them at the door appeared and brought a chair for Guy. Whit kept on eating.

'You're getting fat,' Red said. 'It doesn't become you.'

'You come up here to tell me that?'

'No. I hate to see a man let himself go. They'll get you back in shape in Alcatraz.'

'Always the jester,' said Whit acidly.

'But the cap is getting pretty shabby and the bells lose their merry tinkle. Being pushed around does that.'

'When a man has a reputation for truth he should live up to it.'

134

'One little lie shouldn't count.' Red smiled his thanks to the elderly man for the piece of melon he put in front of him. 'I told you I couldn't find her. I offered you back the fee. How was I to know you couldn't trust her when it came to money? That's what burned you most, wasn't it? The fifty-odd grand?'

'That and a misplaced faith,' said Sterling.

'But why be so devious?' Red asked. 'You went at it in such a round-about way. Getting back at me, I mean.'

'Mind letting me run my life in my own way?'

'Yes,' said Red. 'Because you're not running it any longer.'

The veins on Sterling's short, thick neck stood out and he shot a murderous glance at Parker. 'I should have known you'd slip up. You and Lou. You fumbling, inept bastards!'

'Don't pick on Guy,' Red said. 'He did his best. Look at the cops who are suddenly fond of me. An artistic frame hand carved, Whit. It doesn't become me. That's why I'm here.'

'Yeah, pick on Lou,' Guy said. 'He's the one let Red get his hands on that stuff.'

'I traded him a couple of Bibles for it.' Red took a last mouthful of melon and put his spoon carefully down on the plate. Coffee steamed in his cup and he poured cream in and watched the thick cream lace the black fluid with pale threads. 'Didn't he tell you?'

Whit pushed himself up, puffing out his cheeks. Remembering the thin, dark, esthetic man who long ago had sent him in search of Mumsie, Red thought, you can't touch pitch forever and stay clean. You can't muck around in sewers.

'Sit down,' Red suggested. 'You'll get heartburn. And stop worrying about those records of your indiscretions. You can have them back.'

'You Irish –'

'Not Irish. Welsh. Remove the frame and you can have them.'

Whit settled back in his chair, staring without interest at

135

the poached eggs and ham in front of him. He pushed the plate away.

'I'm not going to be greedy,' Red went on. 'The cash settlement can be modest. The government would give me a third – I think that's what you get for helping the taxpayers. Or maybe it's a half. That racket of Eels' was a good one.'

'Go on.' Whit pushed the words through his thick lips. 'Needle me. Keep on needling me and, you son of a bitch, you'll never get out of here.'

Guy warned Red with a glance but it went unheeded.

'You can't put pride in the bank,' Red smiled gently. 'You can't run your fingers through it or count it. It's hard to swallow – until you start thinking in millions. That sort of helps it to go down.'

'Stop talking crap and speak your piece,' Whit said.

Red gave his attention to his food, eating hungrily, glancing now and then at Whit and at Guy, both silent, both waiting, the one toadlike, the other loosely coiled. Out on the lake a speedboat drew a curving line on the smooth paper-surface of the water. In the tree beyond the porch a squirrel noisily took a sugar-pine cone apart.

'Guy isn't going to like this,' Red said at last. 'Guy is in love and Guy has lost all sense of proportion.'

Guy's hand moved for his pocket.

'I took it – remember?' Red asked. 'The heart wound heals. The yen fades.'

'No,' Guy cried out.

'Guy would even double-cross a man for love,' Red said. 'A new phase. A dangerous one.'

Whit transferred his beady-eyed malevolence to Parker. Whit said, 'That's why you didn't tell me.'

'He's lying.' The words came from a dry throat. Guy wet his lips and studied his knuckles.

'Perhaps I figured you out wrong,' said Red. 'I was under the impression you wanted Mumsie. So it was the small investment after all.'

Guy's chair legs scraped the floor as he pushed it back.

'Sit still,' Red warned him. 'I can take you both apart. But a gun is simpler.'

The chair stopped moving. Guy propped himself against the back, gripping the seat with whitening hands.

'The cops get Mumsie and Joe Stefanos,' Red said. 'Guy gets his dough back. I get enough to spend my waning years on the cliffs of Acapulco or the beach at Mazatlan. Not much. My wants are few, Whit. And you —' he wagged a finger at Sterling — 'you gain a world. Pages and pages of beautiful figures. Freedom. All this — a view of a lake instead of San Francisco Bay.' He rose. 'I'll go out on the porch and watch the squirrels and let you talk it over. Guy's good at frames, Whit. Let him figure out the best way to take the cops off my tail.' He smiled, stepped through the low window and crossed the porch to the steps. He sat down with his back to them.

Clouds formed in the north, struggling with a wind that seemed intent on keeping the sky neat. He'd miss these clouds and he'd miss these hills but there would be other clouds and other hills. And there would be Ann. If she'd have him, there would be Ann. If not? He didn't know the answer to that question. He didn't want to know.

Behind him footsteps crossed the stones. He stood up and turned. Guy wore his mask again. Whit was sullenly resigned.

'All right,' Whit said. 'How much?'

'Fifty thousand.'

'I haven't got it here.'

'Get it.'

'Tonight. I'll have to go to Reno. Where's the file?'

'It will be mailed to you.'

'No.'

'Yes,' Red said. 'I crossed you once. I know better than to try it a second time. I've a reason for living. I've a reason for wanting to be let alone. So you'll get it. But not until I'm out of reach.'

The fat on Whit's shoulders quivered in a shrug. 'That's it then.'

Red nodded. 'I'll pick up the dough late tonight or early tomorrow. Keep a couple of grand back and get me a plane – you must know a pilot who can keep his mouth shut. Have him set it down tomorrow at nine in the meadow off the American River road. Before you start up to Echo Pass.'

'It'll be there,' Whit said.

'Don't look so stricken, Guy,' Red said. 'You'll get over her. I did. Come on.' With that he crossed to the far stairs that led down to the waiting car.

# CHAPTER NINETEEN

JIM CALDWELL was lounging in the doorway of the hardware store talking to Ellis Gore when Ann parked her car in front of the Safeway. Caldwell kept on talking but now he wasn't looking at Gore. He was watching Ann as she got out of the car and crossed the sidewalk, trim and cool in white shorts and white blouse.

Gore's wise old eyes sized up the situation. He said he'd better quit wasting time and get back to work – he had a lot of bills to mail out, he said. Not that it did any good because people paid him when they got around to it.

'See you around,' Caldwell said absently. Then, elaborately casual, he sauntered across to the store and pushed through the turnstile. He didn't see her at first because she was squatting in front of the spice shelf trying to find a can of black pepper. He looked up and down the aisles, knowing that his neck was getting red, knowing that Mrs. Pringle, the gaunt, gray-haired woman at the check stand, saw through him. He knew that within an hour all her cronies would be in possession of this dramatic tidbit. Yes, sir – he comes walking in tryin' not to look like he was followin' her, she would say, licking her thin lips. To hell with her! Caldwell thought. Throwing aside all pretense he went boldly toward the back. Ann stood up, saw him and held out the heavy basket.

Caldwell took it from her and felt good again. This was as it should be – moving along beside her while she pulled cans and boxes from the shelves and dropped them in the basket. One of these days she'd be using his money. One of these days she'd be going home with him and he'd carry the carton full of groceries into the kitchen and help her put the stuff in the cupboards. Winter would be best, coming in out of the snow to the bright warm room that would smell of spices and wood smoke.

For something to say Caldwell asked, 'How's Canby?' He had talked to Miller half an hour before.

'He's fine.' Ann put a box of soap powder in the basket, consulted her list. 'That's everything.'

'Looks like the Miller family's going to eat for a while anyway,' Caldwell said. 'You ought to keep a packmule just to go shopping with. Lead him around and fill up the kyacks.' He put the basket on the check stand, and with a glance told Mrs. Pringle to go ahead and gossip her goddamned head off because what did he care? Sure he loved Ann. Sure he followed her around like an old dog grateful for a careless pat on the head. But it wouldn't always be this way.

The forefinger of Mrs. Pringle's skinny right hand punched the keys on the tabulator while her left hand fished the groceries from the basket. 'It sure is nice to have a man around,' Mrs. Pringle said. 'A man who don't mind helping you shop. That'll be five-sixty-two. How's your mother, Ann? She looked sort of peaked last night.'

Ann put a ten-dollar vill in Mrs. Pringle's hand. 'Mother's all right.'

'Saw her at the movie,' Mrs. Pringle said. 'Her and Canby. Here, Jimmy, make yourself useful and put the stuff in this carton like a good boy.'

Caldwell packed the carton, carried it out and put it on the rear seat of the sedan. Through the door he could see Mrs. Pringle watching them and he thought, The old bitch, the skinny, nosy old bitch! Why can't she keep her nose out of things? That was the trouble with towns like Bridgeport. Everybody tried to live your life for you.

Maybe he was wrong to buy the Carlisle place, maybe it

would be better to go to L.A. or Reno and have people around who didn't give a damn who you were or what you did.

'Thanks, Jimmy.' Ann brushed her hair back and smiled up at him.

'I was thinking,' Caldwell said awkwardly. 'Maybe you don't have to hurry home. Maybe we could run up and see how things are coming along at my new place.'

She wanted to say no. She wanted to say, 'Jimmy, it's no good hoping or planning because tonight I'll push through the willows and he'll be waiting by the creek.'

'It'll only take a few minutes.'

Ann didn't look at him. She didn't dare look at him because she knew her eyes would tell him. 'All right.'

He went around and got in beside her. He let one arm rest on the cushion so that his stubby fingers touched her shoulder. As they drove away he sent one challenging glance at Mrs. Pringle. Let the old bitch talk her head off.

The sun was a blessing and the wind a promise. Tonight – where the creek turned under the fence into the Miller pasture and the willows walled in a tiny stretch of sand. Hurry, sun, her mind said. Hurry down the sky and hide behind the hills.

'I'm going hunting next week,' she heard Caldwell say.

'That's fine.'

'Why don't you come along?'

'We'll see.'

'You got to watch your step these days,' Caldwell said, 'if you want to keep living. More guys around who'll shoot at anything.' He rambled on, talking about things like guns and ridges where the big bucks lay, hills they had climbed and creeks they had followed before a man called Red Bailey had come along to wake him from a dream.

The car turned off the highway and he got out and opened the gate. He stood looking at the big house while she drove through and waited for him. Solid. Built for keeps. Like his love for Ann. Love had started when he was a freshman in high school and she had the seat in front of him. From that day on she had been his girl. The memory of all those years gave him back his confidence. He'd get his dream back. He'd get his world back.

They could hear the pounding of hammers and the hum of a power saw as they drove into the yard. He led her across the porch, smug in his renewed self-confidence. He took her from room to room and her exclamations of pleased surprise at the changes were like sweet balm. A fireplace was taking shape in the kitchen. New windows let the sunlight in. New windows framed the mighty wall of the Sierras and the lush, green carpet of the great meadow. Down by the creek a bulldozer gnawed a hole in the black loam. Soon the hole would be a tiled swimming pool. The fences no longer sagged. They were trim, white, mathematical patterns.

The stone mason grinned and said hello. The two carpenters – old men Caldwell had known all his life – told Ann she was looking mightly pretty, then soberly accepted as their due her words of praise. They were glad she liked the way the place was shaping up. They were sure she was going to be mighty happy here.

Then Jim Caldwell knew. Her eyes told him. Her flushed face told him.

'Come on,' he said coldly, heading for the door. 'I better be getting back.'

Tom Douglas sucked at his cold pipe and looked across at Caldwell. 'Tonight you think?'

'I'll know for sure if the Kid goes fishing,' Caldwell said, his eyes hard and angry.

'He'll lead us to Red?'

'No. Away from Red. So we string along. Some of your boys and some of the state coppers take out after him. Let him think we're being played for suckers. You and the rest of your boys and the rest of the cops stick around the radio. I'll take one of the state cars and when I give you the go signal on the radio you close in.'

142

'It's worth trying.'

'Maybe it won't be tonight,' Caldwell said. 'Maybe it will be tomorrow or the next day. But it will be soon.'

Douglas found pity for the big, awkward fellow sitting taut and desperate in the chair beyond the desk. Tough. To love a girl and know she's going to be in another man's arms pretty soon. To have so much hatred in you you could taste it.

That morning Douglas had been driving in the hills and had seen a coyote sitting in the brush just off the road, so spent he had no fear left in him. Douglas had drawn his gun but his finger would not pull the trigger. He had driven away. Now he thought of the coyote and he thought of Red and wondered if, finding the man in the trap, he would want to let him go. A hell of a business this. Passing judgment – when who were you to judge? And what would it get Jim Caldwell? Would it clear the road? Would it return to him something he had lost? Douglas thought not.

'You sure this is the best way to handle it?' Douglas asked.

'It's the only way,' Caldwell replied.

'We'll give her a whirl then,' Douglas said.


The sun was behind the ridge when the Kid locked up the station and got his roadster out. He drove slowly through town, past the highway patrol station and the sheriff's office. As he headed for the sharp turn south he kept looking into the rearview mirror. He grinned as he saw the sheriff's car pull out from the side of the building and stop in front of the office. They had seen him. Pretty soon they'd be moseying along after him and he'd give them a run for their money. He'd lead them so far away from town they wouldn't get back until midnight. His lips shaped themselves for a whistle and his mind made gay and silent music. His mind imagined sounds – water leaping over rocks, wind running light-footed through a forest. Then the music died because he thought of Ann and Red who knew what love was. Not for him. No love for him anywhere in the silent waste that was his world.

Far behind him a black sedan loaded with armed men and a white and black car with three state coppers in it followed and then, glancing in the mirror, he saw them sneaking along his trail.

Night drained the color from the sky and for a while the mountain range was a ragged outline against the darkening wall of nothingness. Then it became part of the darkness.

A car pulled out from behind the state highway patrol office and headed west, lightless, driven by a thick-set young man in a green uniform. Before it reached the Miller place it swung into a lane, south a mile, then along another to stop by a watering trough where a dozen cattle slept. Jim Caldwell got out, climbed through the fence and made his way cautiously through the pasture. As he came nearer the house he heard the blat of the radio. Canby would be sitting by it reading and Ann and Mrs. Miller would be in the kitchen washing dishes.

The dog barked once. Smelling a familiar scent it came up to him and nosed one hand. Jim tugged the soft ears and sent him back to the front porch with a whispered order. He went around back of the house and entered the woodshed. From his hiding place he could see into the kitchen with Ann standing at the sink. The sight of her sharpened the bright blade of his anger.

Mrs. Miller moved from the sink to the cupboard putting the dishes away. Every now and then she went to the doorway that led into the living room to tell Canby to turn that thing down – you could hear it all the way to Reno. If Canby heard her, he was not impressed because the radio kept right on blatting.

Hunched down in his musty hiding place Caldwell wished Canby would shut the thing off. Then he could hear Ann's voice.

The last dish was placed in the rack. Ann scrubbed the

sink board and the sink. She dried her hands on a dish towel, took off her apron and hung it on the hook back of the stove. She faced her mother. Her lips moved and Mrs. Miller's flat, hard voice rose above the blare of the music.

'Can't you ever stay home?' Mrs. Miller mourned.

Suddenly the radio was silent. Canby appeared in the doorway. 'Let her alone,' Canby said, 'If she wants to go out, she has a right to, goddamn it.'

'Don't swear,' said Mrs. Miller.

'I'm only going for a walk,' Ann said.

'Seems like you'd get enough walking daytimes,' Mrs. Miller complained.

'Do I try to run your life? Ann asked.

'Why should you?'

'Run along,' Canby told his daughter. 'We're going to the movies anyway.'

'We went last night,' Mrs. Miller said.

'So we went last night,' Canby replied and turned back into the living room. 'Get your hat on.'

Jim Caldwell's eyes saw nothing in the drab domestic scene to wonder at, nothing to make him consider even momentarily the thought that people got old and people took each other for granted and presently there was no magic in the world. Jesus, she was beautiful standing there under the hard, white light, her head tilted a little, her cheeks flushed, her dark eyes full of stars. She blew a kiss after her father, gave her mother a dutiful peck on the cheek and came out into the back yard. She stopped for a moment to hunt for star patterns through the trees. She followed the path through the gate into the pasture, her step quickened. Jim Caldwell knew only a deep and sullen hatred for everyone.

A night bird cried out. The sound – the distilled essence of all loneliness – had no sadness in it for Ann. The creek talked quietly to itself and a faint murmuring arose in the willows as the wind pushed through. Up on the ridge a coyote yapped shrilly. Another and another set the canyons echoing with their wailing. Below, the dogs answered. Presently deciding that their tame brothers had been annoyed enough, the coyotes stopped yelling. Quiet reigned again.

Ann sat on the warm sand, her ears strained to catch the first faint sound of his approach. Something moved in the willows across the creek and she sat forward wanting to call out but not daring to. Quiet again. The creek chuckled at her and she hugged her knees and savored every moment of this night. This world was not empty now. Never empty any more. Oh, precious night! Oh, warm and lovely dark! Splashing sounded in the marshland behind her as he pushed through the screening willows and she was in his arms.

No words at first because there was no need for words.

He drew his face away and said softly, 'Ann, Ann.'

'Darling.' Her palm felt the good roughness of his cheek.

'You didn't forget me?'

'I'll never forget you.'

He dropped on the sand and drew her down beside him. 'Maybe you will.'

'No.'

'Wait.'

'I don't care what you've done,' Ann said.

'You don't believe I've done anything,' Red said. 'That's the trouble.'

'No. I don't care.'

He kissed her again. 'One thing you know is right. I love you. I always will. That's why I'm here. That's why I didn't wait and send for you.'

'I would have come.'

'Sure. Without knowing. Without thinking. So I didn't send for you.'

'Don't tell me anything,' Ann said. 'I don't want to know. I don't want to think.'

'I killed a guy a long time ago,' Red said. Her hand pressed against his lips and he pulled it gently away. 'I fixed it so someone else will get the blame. Now will you follow me?'

'Anywhere.'

146

'Because you don't believe me.'

'Don't talk.'

'My conscience hurts me not at all,' Red said. 'Someday it may, though I doubt it. The man I killed asked for it, deserved it. The one I'm blaming helped build my gallows high. One day you'll look at me and all the things I've done will haunt us.'

Again one hand found his lips and again he took the soft hand away.

'Love's easy to kill,' Red said.

'Not mine.'

'I'm not going to take you with me,' Red said. 'I'm going to leave you with it. A month. Two. Then I'll send for you and I'll want you to come even though I know it will be wrong. I'm taking no chance. You are.'

'I know the answer now.'

'It's the night,' Red said, 'and the hills around us.'

'I'm going with you tonight.'

Red shook his head. 'You're going to listen and then you're going to wait. So shabby, Ann. My soul. Cut from such shoddy goods. Faded and patched and shabby.'

'I like shabby souls,' Ann whispered and put her head against his chest.

He kissed her hair. He said, 'I'm going to Acapulco because that's where it all started and maybe after I've been there a little while I won't ask you to follow me. There was a girl. Crossing a sidewalk into a cafe and into my life –'

'I don't want to hear it.'

'You must. I won't play God. I'm too old and tired and beat up around the edges to be omnipotent. I knew she had shot a man and I knew she was a thief and I didn't care –'

She pressed her head tight against him and felt his strong arms around her. She was listening to him but not wanting to and not caring what he said. Across the creek Jim Caldwell crouched in the grass and the murmur of the creek was not loud enough to drown out Red Bailey's deep voice. Presently Caldwell began inching away, making no sound, moving on

147

hands and knees through the soft wet grass. If Red heard him he was too deep in the past to care.

Fifty yards. A hundred. Then Caldwell stood up and, still cautious, crossed the pasture to the fence, clambered through and, bending low, made his way to the car.

Where was his anger? Where was his hatred? He leaned on the wheel staring into the darkness. Within reach of his hand was a bit of metal and rubber that would bring men with guns to the creek. But he did not reach for it. 'I won't play God,' Red Bailey had said. Well, neither could he. Maybe she'd follow Red Bailey. He wasn't going to stop her. And if she did and if things didn't work out he would be waiting. Not because he was noble but because he was a goddamned fool.

He put his head on his arms and squeezed his eyes tight. He sat up, started the motor and drove slowly back to town.

Tom Douglas watched him come into the circle of light on the porch and through the open door.

'May as well go home,' Caldwell said, fumbling in his pocket for a match. 'The red son of a bitch fooled me. He didn't show up.'

'Too bad,' Tom Douglas said.

# CHAPTER TWENTY

DAWN WAS STILL a long way off but the thin rind of the moon had finally found enough strength to get over the mountains. Now you could see the lake and the sketchy hills. Red drove carefully, fighting sleep, fighting the weariness that numbed his mind. He was not happy though he should have been. Ann had heard him through and Ann had said that nothing mattered. She'd wait and when he sent for her she'd follow him – the past no secret now, the web they had spun for him soon swept away. Freedom of a sort. Would it work? If not, a bright moment or two. And that's about all you were entitled to – more than most men had. 'Send for me soon,' Ann had said. 'So very soon, darling.'

His eyes closed a moment. He slapped himself awake, pulled the car back to the road, and turned the wind wing so the cold air poured through. He was on the lake road now, rounding Emerald Bay. A mile more, then the turn. Maybe Whit had changed his mind. Maybe Whit would be waiting for him with a gun. He hoped not. Seeing the opening in the tree wall he turned up the graveled drive.

The iron gates were open. Wide open. He stopped and switched off the lights. He was thoroughly awake now. One hand sought the gun in his pocket. Warily he walked through, looking all around him and up at the lighted windows. No gate-keeper. No sound but the wind in the trees and the crunch of gravel underfoot.

Because there was so much at stake Red knew what fear

was, as he followed the winding drive to stop under the porte-cochere and looked through an open door into the hall.

An open door. An empty hallway. Why? On the hill above, the trees rubbed shoulders and whispered to each other. He wanted to turn away and climb up to them, away from the emptiness and the silence. He took his gun from his pocket and looked at it. He thought, this isn't going to do me any good. They'll be waiting for me inside and that will be it. Then he stepped through the open door, to be stopped, not by a bullet, but by Joe Stefanos' body sprawled at the foot of the staircase. The little Greek had been shot through the head.

All wrong, he thought. Joe shouldn't be dead. Joe should be waiting in the living room with a gun in his fist.

But there he was, as dead as Lloyd Eels, as dead as Meta Carson. Life even caught up with guys like Joe Stefanos.

And to guys like Whit Sterling – which didn't surprise him. He had expected, when he saw the open door, to find Sterling's body kicking around somewhere. He found it. It lay face down in front of the fireplace in the big room that looked out on the lake and death wasn't kind enough to give Whit Sterling dignity. A messy lump of flesh – and what would the Treasury Department care now?

Well, build the gallows higher. You couldn't frame a dead man and you couldn't make deals with a dead man. The web was spun more intricately, more perfectly than ever.

Standing above the body of the man who could have given him freedom, Red knew the spinner of that web.

Mumsie gave up her dream reluctantly – her eyes closed against the unwelcome light, shivering a little, yet not awake enough to cover her lovely body.

'Guy?' she asked.

Lack of an answer didn't bother her. She stretched, opened her eyes and saw Red Bailey standing by the bed.

'The window was open,' Red said.

She drew the sheet around her and sat up, not serene now, knowing what fear was.

'Don't yell,' Red said. 'It won't do you any good.'

'You shouldn't be here,' she said foolishly.

'I walked knee-deep in blood to get here,' Red said. 'Joe's blood and Whit Sterling's blood. An abattoir, Mumsie.'

She wet her lips. She shivered and pulled the sheet tighter.

'Dig deep, Mumsie. Find horror and put it in your eyes.'

'Red –'

'I'm going to Acapulco,' Red said. 'Remember, Mumsie – the cliffs and the sky and the buzzards wheeling over. I'll watch them wheel. I'll watch their shadows on the rocks.'

'Let me alone,' she whimpered.

'Don't you want to go with me?'

'Go away.'

'You ran from death once.'

'I didn't –'

'Where is it?' His voice grew sharp.

'Make sense, Red.' She tried to find tears for him.

'Don't. You've lost your touch. Where is it?' He bent over her, dug his fingers in her shoulder.

'Guy –'

'Not Guy.'

'He'll come soon.'

'Let him. I'll hand him a gun and I'll say, 'Kill her because I can't. God knows why, but I can't.' His fingers dug deeper. 'Where?'

'Don't.' Her sudden glance betrayed her.

He thrust her down and moved around the bed to the closet. Shoved far back in the corner was a small traveling case. He picked it up, came back into the room and, seeing the look on her face, he smiled. 'Finally you're afraid,' he said.

'Put it down.'

'You weren't afraid when through the window you watched Joe kill Whit Sterling. You weren't afraid when you slipped

through an open door. That little hand steady – so very
steady. Was Joe surprised, Mumsie?'

'Put that down,' she yelled.

'You forget. It belongs to me.' He put the bag on the bed,
opened it, took out a packet of bills from the dozens packed
carefully inside, tossed it to her. 'Your cut for collecting from
Whit,' he said.

The money lay on the pillow near the headboard. Her
hand reached for it. But her fingers didn't close over the
neat little packet. Instead her hand went under the pillow and
he saw the flash of metal. He felt himself pushed backward as
the bullet hit him in the chest. Then he was on her and he
had the gun.

He watched her crawl across the bed to where the open
case was. Very slowly he went over and pried her fingers
loose. As he put the case under his left arm he saw blood
staining his white shirt. Behind him the door opened and
turning he saw Guy.

'Come in and close the door,' Red said. 'It's all right. I'm
the one got shot.'

Guy looked at the gun in Red's hand and he looked at the
woman on the bed. He came in and closed the door.

'Such a greedy little bitch,' Red said. 'I'm afraid she's
going to give you a bad time of it.'

Mumsie wasn't looking at Guy. Mumsie wasn't listening.
She was staring at the little case tucked under Red's arm
and slowly she swung off the bed and started across the
room.

'No. You can't have it,' Mumsie said dully.

'See how greedy?' Red said as he pushed her away.

Guy started toward him, but stopped because Red was
motioning with his gun.

'You'll be happier if you let the cops have her, Guy. An
empty bed is better than a coffin.'

'What in hell are you talking about?' Guy cried.

'She killed Joe Stefanos.'

Guy went to her, shook her. 'You didn't go to Reno. You lied.'

'No. She didn't go to Reno. She went with Joe to Tahoe. Joe shot Whit and she shot Joe and then she ran off with my money.'

'Goddamn you!' Guy cried. 'Oh, goddamn you!'

'Goodbye,' Red said. 'Don't be too bitter. We were trying to pin a murder on her.' He opened the door, closed it carefully behind him and walked slowly down the hall to the stairs. Save for the paunchy man called Mac the hall was empty. Mac stood at the foot of the steps frowning up at him and because Red had a gun he didn't let out a yell.

So many stairs, Red thought, as he went slowly down – so many for a man as tired as he was. Mustn't drop the little bag. He and Ann needed what was in it. Mustn't let anyone stop him. Mac was right in front of him now.

'Go on,' Red said. 'Go through the front door.'

Mac wasn't looking at him. Mac was looking past him up the stairs at Guy on the landing.

'Go on. Never mind about Guy,' Red told him.

But Mac didn't move so Red went past him to the open door, across the veranda and down the steps.

He stumbled as he crossed the graveled drive and the case slid from under his arm. He looked down at it. Then he knew there was no use picking it up. It wasn't going to do him any good. Nothing was going to do him any good. This was it and maybe that was how it should be. Maybe? No question about it. Jack Fisher dead and Lloyd Eels dead and Meta Carson dead and who was there to tell the cops he didn't kill them all? Anyway, a lot of guys who deserved to die were corpses. Anyway, the web now held Guy Parker and a woman named Mumsie McGonigle. He hoped Ann wouldn't mind too much.

The sky flamed about the mountain wall where clouds were piled. He'd miss those hills, he thought. He'd miss those clouds. *Look up once more. Up. Up.*

He didn't hear the gun when Guy shot him because he was dead.

# b l u e   m u r d e r

| | | | |
|---|---|---|---|
| ☐ | 65270 2 | **WILLIAM P. MCGIVERN** The Big Heat | £3.50 |
| ☐ | 65278 8 | **DAVIS GRUBB** The Night of the Hunter | £3.50 |
| ☐ | 65275 3 | **CHARLES WILLIAMS** The Diamond Bikini | £3.50 |
| ☐ | 65266 4 | **DAVID GOODIS** The Burglar | £3.50 |
| ☐ | 65280 X | **JOEL TOWNSLEY ROGERS** The Red Right Hand | £3.95 |
| ☐ | 65269 9 | **CORNELL WOOLRICH** Rear Window and Other Stories | £4.50 |
| ☐ | 65281 8 | **NEWTON THORNBURG** Cutter and Bone | £3.95 |
| ☐ | 65282 6 | **GEOFFREY HOMES** Build My Gallows High | £3.95 |
| ☐ | 65279 6 | **GIL BREWER** 13 French Street & The Red Scarf | £4.50 |

All these books are available at your local bookshop or newsagent, or can be ordered direct from the publisher. Just tick the titles you want and fill in the form below.

Prices and availability subject to change without notice.

Blue Murder Paperbacks, P.O. Box 11, Falmouth, Cornwall.

Please send cheque or postal order, and allow the following for postage and packing:

U.K. – 60p for one book, plus 25p for the second book, and 15p for each additional book ordered up to a maximum of £1.90.

Overseas (including EIRE) – £1.25 for the first book, plus 75p for the second, and 28p for each additional book thereafter.

Name............................................................................................................

Address.......................................................................................................

..........................................................................................................